# Ghostly Bounty

EILEEN MAKI

ISBN: 1491030496
ISBN-13: 978-1491030493

# DEDICATION

This book is dedicated to those I love, who more extraordinary than any tale of the paranormal. I love you.

And to those who believe that life exists beyond our knowledge and the earthly plane of existence.

~ Eileen

# CONTENTS

# NOTE FROM THE AUTHOR

The events in this story are based on an actual experience that were told to me by the person who had the adventure. Portions of this text are his actual words as he told them to me. It is my hope that as you read this story, you hear his voice and come to know and understand his personality and his heart. Feel what he felt as he was lead through this journey by a supernatural force. This story really happened, to a real person, in a real house. Enjoy!

# DISCLAIMER

Although the events of this story are real, the names of the characters are not. Any resemblance to actual persons, either living or dead, is purely coincidental. The names have been changed to protect the confidentiality and privacy of those involved.

# INTRODUCTION

Dear Reader,

I wanted to write a little introduction to give you some information about me. I want you to know that I am a regular, down to earth person. So without wasting any more time, here's a little bit about me.

I grew up in Portland's East County. Raised a Catholic, I transitioned to a non-denominational Christian in my later years and my faith remained strong into my adult life. As with a lot of Christians who are strong in their faith, I did not believe in spirits or ghosts. I certainly put no stock into stories of hauntings and thought Mediums were rip-off artists.

I never believed that dead loved ones could be contacted, and I most certainly never imagined that I would be chosen to convey a message from beyond the grave.

The story you are about to read is true. It really happened in the way it is portrayed. Though names have been changed to protect the identities of those involved, the story is told to the best of my ability and as accurate as I can recall.

Keep in mind, as you read my tale, that I am just a regular person. I have a family and a job; I believe in God and have friends. Just like you. Imagine if you were the one who experienced these events as they occurred. What choice would you have made? Would you have made the same choices I did? And how would this experience have changed your life? Because let me assure you, it certainly changed mine.

Sincerely,

Larry Campbell

# PART 1: THE MONEY

# CHAPTER ONE

I had been searching for the right investment for months with no luck. All of my offers had been out-bid or rejected and I was starting to feel as if I had made the wrong decision when I chose to start down this path. I felt my dreams slipping away and I felt like all my hard work and planning was for nothing. I was going to end up right where I started; in debt, with nothing.

I'm just a regular guy. I'm really no different than anybody else. I am pretty strong in my Christian faith; I have a couple of great kids, and a pretty good career. I really am just a normal person trying to work hard and realize my dreams. Like others who work hard and have dreams, finances always seemed to somehow get out of control and to stand in the way of my goals and aspirations. No matter how hard I tried to save and spend frugally, I was always robbing Peter to pay Paul and living paycheck to paycheck. During one of my planning stages where I would sit down and plan out my budget, plan my spending, figure out what the family needed and decide to stick to it this time, I remembered about a system I had heard about a few years back. It was a very famous and popular financial system I had heard about. I did a little research to refresh myself on the details and then I bought the book and listened to the videos and audio files. The system the financial expert had put together made some pretty good common sense. I had never really been taught how to manage money or do personal budgets, so hearing for the first time that there is a process and a tried and true method for getting out of debt and taking control of my life was exciting for me. I was eager to put the system to good use.

So, here, in the beginning of my story, I want to make it clear that money and I have never been strangers. In my life, I have made good money, and I have spent good money, just like everybody else. That is one of the most interesting twists to this story. My experience with money had always been personal and on a moderate scale. But no matter what I had dealt with in the past, little did I know that it was not going to be quite enough to prepare me for what was about to happen. I don't think anything really could have prepared me for what was about to happen.

My wife and I reviewed the financial system materials, discussed our options and decided to go for it. Following the financial system philosophy and system, we sold off all of our toys and paid off all of our credit accounts, including our cars. We cut up all of our credit cards. I had recently sold a business and had made a big enough profit from that sale that I was in a pretty good position to be able to concentrate on the debt free path we had committed to. It was all starting to come together and we were really accomplishing those goals we had set for ourselves. We were feeling good and really excited about how things were working out. The financial system we were following advised us to have at least six months' worth of expenditures in emergency savings in the bank so that was one of the first goals we checked off our list. We put that money into an account and didn't touch it. That was for emergencies. We also set money aside for the kids' college funds. With these goals met, we were in pretty good shape. We didn't have any debt except the mortgage on our home and we were feeling pretty wonderful about the whole thing.

I grew up in and around the construction business. Over the course of my life, I had owned a couple of contracting businesses. When house flipping started becoming so popular and so widespread and gaining so much publicity, I started to look for a house to invest in. I wanted to buy the house and put my construction experience and background to good use. Of course, the purpose of house flipping is to make a profit, so I was hoping my experience would help me make the necessary changes to the house I bought so I could sell it for a profit. The ultimate goal was to make strides to pay off my mortgage. Only then would me and my family truly be debt free. Well, that was the plan anyway. I talked about the plans with my family, I prayed about it and I looked at lots and lots of houses. It seemed that every single house either already had an offer accepted before I could get mine in or there was a better offer than mine, or it was a cash offer. I made between 15 and 20 unsuccessful offers before I started to feel discouraged. I had looked at about 50 homes, spent hours and hours of time looking, driving, estimating, and dreaming. I was feeling discouraged but I was also pretty anxious to get something I could invest in. I was eager to get started on my plan to be debt free. For some reason, it just wasn't happening for me. My career allowed me to have days off sometimes and work nights and I usually had weekends off. I talked with friends and family about my plan, I prayed about it constantly, I thought about it constantly and dreamed of the success I could bring to me and my family when the plan finally panned out. I was looking at upwards of 6 houses each day in addition to working my full-time job. I was getting worn out and starting to feel like I had made the wrong investment choice. Maybe this plan wasn't the right plan for me and my family.

The days came and went and even though I remained optimistic, the opportunity to shine was looking more and more like the opportunity to make the wrong decision. On a day like any other, I came across a house that demanded my attention. It was just a monster of a house at a little over 4,500 square feet. My Realtor and I pulled up to the house just before lunch. There were already several cars in the driveway and more parked on the street near the house.

Getting out of the car, I surveyed the house and yard. The house was a low slung beauty with a fenced in patio and backyard area. There were large concrete steps leading up to the double front doors which was framed with slim windows and large potted plants. The front yard was landscaped with lush green grass on one side and bark and rock formations on the other. There were big bay windows in the front and an attached garage off to the side.

We entered the house, and as I walked in, I felt like the sun was beaming down on me. The sheer size of the structure was overwhelming at first but as I walked through the house, walked the halls and stairs, I began to see that the house had a lot of potential. Everything about the house caught my attention. With each room I moved into, I felt more and more excited; more and more like this was the one, this was the house I had to choose. We did the walk through and stepped outside onto the front walkway. My Realtor waited outside while I went back through the house again. This time, I took more time. I walked through the house, shutting out the milling people, their conversations and cell phones. There were people inside the house, there were people outside the house, there were people in the backyard, people on their phones as I walked by. I could hear them talking, "Hey, call Jim and call me right back. You won't believe this house!"

I tuned them out as I looked, walking almost in a daze through the entire house again. It was just incredible. I was in awe. It was like I was on an unguided tour through a historical home museum. It was as if the walls spoke to me. I could instantly visualize every single room, every facet of that house. I felt the warmth here and I felt my dream coming back to life. I smiled to myself as I walked toward the front door where my Realtor waited for me. I had never experienced that before. With all the houses I had looked at, this was the very first time I had ever found myself actually emotionally involved in a house. Here I was, getting more and more excited about this house and I had already broken the cardinal rule of house flipping: don't get emotionally involved. The rules said to treat it like a business, because of course, it was a business. Plan carefully, see the profit and move on to the next one. Don't get emotionally involved with the houses. I stepped outside and joined my Realtor on the walkway. Feeling overwhelmed with thoughts and emotions, I got into his car.

I looked at the house as we pulled away from the curb and a tidal wave of something washed over me. It was exhilaration, it was joy, it was sadness and love all at once. I blinked as the sun pierced my eyes and then the feeling was gone.

Down the street from the house, there was a little coffee shop. My Realtor, Sam, and I went to grab a cup of coffee and talk about my options with the house. Sam knew how much I wanted to finally get started on a house and he could also tell how very excited about this house I truly was.

"I really like this house, Sam, what do you recommend I offer?" I asked him, sipping my steaming coffee.

We had been through this line of questioning many times before with other houses. But as I looked at him pondering my question, I knew in my heart that it didn't matter what he said. This one was mine. I had my personal rules when considering houses. One of them was to, of course, make an offer that was much lower than the asking price.

Sam looked over at me and he said, "Larry, I'm gonna be straight with you because I know how much you want to get started. If you want this house, you need to buy it now. You need to make the offer right now and you need to offer full price. The asking price."

We looked at one another across the bistro table and I knew he was serious. I think, equally, he knew just how serious I was too.

"You need to go with $10,000 earnest money. " He continued. At the time, standard earnest money was around $2,000, nowhere near the $10,000 he was throwing on the table now. "And no inspection," he added.

I could tell by the look on his face that he expected me to be shocked. He expected me to balk, to say 'No, I can't do that.' But it wasn't in me. I had worked with Sam enough to know he was being honest with me, that if I wanted this house I needed to act fast and I needed to break my own rules. The rules hadn't been serving me well up to this point, so I threw my rules out the window.

"Let's do it." I said. There was no hesitation in my voice, no doubt in my heart. I wanted to do this, to get started and to get it done. I was excited and exhilarated. I couldn't wait to get at that house. I wanted that house. I wanted that house like I had never wanted anything before in my life. Sam smiled at me and I grinned back. This was it, I felt it in my bones, a turning point.

We made the offer on a Tuesday and the process started. I offered what Sam had suggested, full asking price, no inspection and $10,000 earnest money. We submitted the offer on Tuesday and we got a verbal response back on Wednesday. My heart sunk when I heard that they already had two other offers that had been submitted before mine. I was anxious, antsy. On Thursday morning, I called to check the status of my offer and was told they would not give out any information until Friday at the earliest.

I was disappointed. I felt that if my offer were going to be accepted, I would have heard by now. The process to purchase would be in motion. I told Sam over the phone, "There goes another one."

Sam expressed his opinion that if they were going to accept our offer, we would have heard by now. I can't tell you how upset I was. I had really thought that was the one. I wrote it off as another failed offer and told Sam to start finding me more houses to look at. Sam called me back in a few hours and we went to look at another three or four houses that same day. Walking through those other houses, I felt empty. They didn't speak to me the way the other house had. They had no music, no life. They were dead structures to me. There was a small flame inside me that still hoped the other offer would come through, that the magical house that made me feel alive would be mine. But to save myself some grief, I let myself make the assumption that this was a repeat of all the previous offers that had been too late, too low or just turned down.

I went home that day feeling like I needed to once again evaluate the plan. Was this the right course of action for me? My wife and I talked that night. We talked about what the options were, investment opportunities that would allow us to continue on with our goal of being debt free, of paying off our mortgage. I went to bed feeling defeated.

Friday morning, my wife and I were in the kitchen when my cell phone rang. We looked at each other. It was fairly early for my cell phone to be ringing. My first thought was that something was wrong, someone was hurt or there was an emergency at work. I answered quickly, without looking at who the caller was.

"Hello? This is Larry." I said, eager to hear the situation.

"Larry!" It was a man's voice. I struggled to place it. "It's Sam."

It was my Realtor. He had never called me this early in the morning before. I had actually wondered if he got out of bed before ten in the morning, but here he was on the phone. And there was something in his voice that made me stand up tall and pay attention to what he was saying.

"Sam?" I said, a little caught off guard, "Is everything alright?"

He sounded flustered, like he was just dying to tell me something but he couldn't get it out, he didn't know how to start.

"Larry," he finally got out, "you're not going to believe this."

"What?" I asked, more curious than ever. My heart started pounding.

"There were two other full-price offers on the house," he began.

"Which house?" I had already written off my dream house, but I hadn't made any other offers since that one so I wasn't sure what he was talking about.

"THE HOUSE." Sam said, excitement in his voice.

I heard his words, but I didn't know why two other full-price offers would have him so flustered and excited. I waited, hoping he would explain himself and start making sense.

"Okay." Was all I could get out. I glanced at my wife who was looking at me as she drank her coffee. She had one eyebrow quirked up over her blue eyes and as I looked at her, she threw a hand up as if to say 'What the heck?' I shrugged and turned my attention back to Sam.

"So they had three full-price offers for that mammoth of a house, Larry. Three."

I waited, assuming he was getting to the point, and he was.

"Three offers, but only one offered $10,000 earnest money. And only one had no inspection." Sam was silent. I could hear him ruffling papers and breathing heavy.

"What does that mean Sam?" It still wasn't sinking in.

His next words stunned me. My wife says I turned three shades of white and she feared I would pass out right there on the kitchen floor.

"We got the house," I said to her.

Sam was still talking on the other end of my cell phone. Sarah and I were just looking at each other. She had stopped, with her coffee cup halfway to her mouth. She began to smile and I smiled back.

"We got the house," we both said at the same time and started laughing.

I suddenly realized Sam was still talking and grabbed a pen to start writing down information. He gave me a few instructions and I went down to his office that afternoon to talk details and sign all the papers. Because of the size of the earnest money and the offer of no inspection, I was already pre-approved. There was no going back now, it was a done deal. It was ours.

We got the house.

# CHAPTER TWO

It took a long six weeks for the closing to be complete. I was a whirlwind of excitement and impatience. Finally the day came and I signed the closing papers on a Wednesday afternoon. Thursday morning I got the keys. I held them in my hands for a moment. They felt heavy, but unlike most keys that haven't been held for a long time, they did not feel cold. I looked down at them in my hands and I swear they were hot. I couldn't believe it was really happening. I simply could not wait to get over to the house and do the walk through. I pulled into the driveway and sat looking at the house for a while. I must have sat there for ten minutes, just looking at the thing. It was huge. It was magnificent. It was mine.

I grabbed the supplies I would need for the walk through. They had been sitting on the seat next to me. I walked towards the front of the house, stepping slowly, savoring the moment. This was it. I was opening the door to my dreams. I held the key in my hand. I inserted the keys in the lock, half expecting them to not work, but they did. I turned the key, feeling the bolt slide back, allowing me entry. There are no words to properly describe how I felt turning that handle for the first time. I opened the door and pushed it inward. Stepping into the entryway, I felt like I was coming home. I had an overwhelming feeling that this was right, that I was meant to be here, right now in this time and space. It was my time and my space.

I must have spent five or six hours at the house that first time, just going through the house room by room. I felt as if each room was a new discovery even though I had seen it before. It felt both homey and new at the same time. It was incredibly comfortable and I felt welcomed inside those walls. The only way I can even come close to describing it completely is that I just fell in love with that house. It really was a beautiful and incredible house.

When I finished the walk through, I stood in the kitchen, making notes on my pad of paper that I put on the counter. And then I began to walk through again. Where would I begin? There were so many thoughts running through my mind. Walking from room to room, my mind was racing, thinking 'I'll tear this out', 'I'll put that in', 'I'll replace that', 'That needs paint', 'I could change that', 'I will need to tear that out', and so forth and so on. Round and round my thoughts were spinning. My heart was racing and my dreams were galloping at full speed like a racehorse finally let out to an open field. My biggest fear was doing too much, spending too much money on the remodel. I had already paid full price on the house which was way more than I had anticipated paying on my first project house. Not to mention that I had now broken the second rule of house flipping: make your money when you buy the house. This, of course, meant to buy low and sell high after the remodeling was done. I thought about it and knew I had done something I hadn't anticipated doing. But somehow, I didn't really seem to be concerned about it. I felt no fear or panic. There was not even a twinge of worry at that point. I stood in the kitchen of that great house and I just had this overwhelming feeling that it was the right thing. This was the right house and I was supposed to be there and I was supposed to have that house. I smiled to myself, knowing that this was it; this was definitely my time to shine. And this was the house that was going to let in the sun.

The shows on TV made things look so easy. But, of course, the TV house flippers had crews of workers, designers, and others helping out. It was just me and my family, but I knew we could do it. I knew I could do it. It was just a matter, at this point, of where to start. I had a big meeting with my family. Everybody came over to the house. I talked about the dream, what we were trying to accomplish with this house and all the hard work we had ahead of us. We were all feeling very excited and ready to get this project underway. We went through the house room by room and everyone was oohing and aahing and throwing out ideas and questions. It was like a meeting of the minds, we were all talking at once and having all these great ideas for the house. That first day I had taken some tools over to the house and my kids were with me too. We went through the house again, as we went through, we started busting out the tile counter top in the kitchen. We didn't finish that, we just got it started, and then we worked in the bathroom, tearing out some of this and some of that. Again, we didn't finish in the bathroom; we just started some activities and then moved on to the living room. We tore out some of the wood paneling that was on the walls in the living room. We were so excited to be there and to get started, we were visualizing all these great ideas and how we would accomplish the look we wanted for the rooms, that we sort of went through the house like a tornado. Our work that day was a total hodgepodge, some stuff done in the kitchen, the bathroom, a bedroom or two, but nothing complete and nothing was really planned out completely. As we were storming our way through the house, in my mind, I was thinking about how much money we were going to make when we got all done and sold the house. I had paid so much for it and planned so many updates and renovations that I was sure the house would sell for much more than I had paid for it.

I remembered about a set of audio books a friend of mine had given me just shortly before I had purchased and listened to the financial system tapes. The book was written by a woman author and had some inspirational title. It was about the laws of attraction and how you can bring positive things to you if you are positive and work towards being positive and making good things happen. The book is based on a three-step process that if you ask and believe it will happen, you will receive your dreams. And by being grateful for what you receive, you will receive favor with the universe and with God and will continue to receive good things. As I was going through the house, I was thinking about the success we would realize when it was all said and done, the profits we would make, the money, the money, and the money we would realize from the sale of the house. It was an interesting concept that the power of my thoughts could bring success and profit to me and my family.

As I mentioned earlier, my family and I had not been in a very good position financially in quite some time. However, following our new plan to success, I had just sold my business, paid off all of our debt, set aside a sizable emergency savings and had also set up a sizable savings account. We had no real debt except for the mortgage on our home. It was truly an amazing feeling to know that the only monthly payments we had to make were our house payment and the regular utility and house related bills to keep our lights on, water running and food on the table. Having watched house flipping reality shows on TV many times and thinking to myself 'I could do that, it looks easy', and with my remodeling and construction background, it seemed like a no-brainer, it seemed like everything was working in our favor and we were on the right track to success. I had prayed about it, thought about it, planned it out, anticipated the work I would need to put in to make it work, and I had done all the things I was supposed to do. I was feeling confident and I knew we were in pretty good shape to make this work and to make our dreams come true. Things were finally moving forward and I was very excited. After having so many offers turned down or beat out and then feeling so good about this house and having it all come together, it just seemed like there was a greater purpose in mind. At the time, I thought it was the power of positive thought bringing what I had asked for into my lap. I wasn't sure if I believed that one hundred percent, but it was clear to me, even then that something was in the driver's seat, making sure I made all the right turns and didn't stop at any red lights.

It was hard for me to gather my thoughts into a clear and concrete plan of action for the house. We were all so excited and feeding off the enthusiasm of one another, almost like we were possessed. We started in a kind of haphazard manner. I found it funny that we couldn't stop for just a moment to gather our thoughts, we just forged ahead and I wasn't worried a bit. I knew it would all turn out alright. As we went from room to room, I would have a pretty clear idea, a mental picture of what I wanted to do in that particular room. But by the time I circled back to that room again, my thought process had changed and now I had a whole new set of ideas and pictures of what that room would look like when it was all finished. I was constantly asking myself, 'What am I going to use this room for?' and 'How much are we going to do in here?', 'How little are we going to do in this room?' and other such questions. I was continually evaluating each room and what I wanted to keep and what I wanted to change. It was no longer one clear picture, but an ever changing Rolodex of visions and ideas. I found that the more I worked in the house and the more I brainstormed ideas that most of the rooms just would not fall into a solid plan. I wanted to write down the plan for the rooms and draw some rough sketches and so forth. But I just found myself wavering on making the final decision of what those rooms would look like at the end. This wasn't like me. I usually had such a clear plan of what to do; I was puzzled as to why I couldn't finalize the plans on most of the rooms. Despite the general indecision, there were three rooms in particular that I knew for sure what I was going to do with them: the kitchen, the upstairs main bathroom, and the smaller room in the basement.

With the kitchen, I knew I only wanted to really redo the counter tops and the floor and leave in the original cabinets. The upstairs main bathroom was the only functional bathroom in the house at this time. It had old style tile work that went up the walls about five feet. The floor was tiled, the counter tops were tiled, the walls were tiled. This was a lot of tile, but it looked very classy. It was the authentic original design and I loved how it looked, so I was trying to preserve that at all costs. However, I still wanted to update the plumbing, the sinks, the tub, and put a shower stall in there. That would be a challenge to do without ruining all that authentic tiling. The other room that I thought I knew exactly what I wanted to do with was a room in the basement. At the bottom of the stairs to the basement, there was a small room to the right. It was at the end of the hall. The room was sort of an odd shape. It was small and only had one small window. It also had no closet. In my mind, it would be the perfect size for a bedroom, but a bedroom needed a closet. The hall outside the room extended past the room's door about another eight feet but did not go anywhere. The hallway dead ended against the wall. My thought was that we should put a new wall just past the bedroom door in the hallway. This would close off that portion of the hallway that dead ended against the wall. Then, if we cut a doorway inside the room going into the now closed off hallway, that part of the hallway could then be used as a closet for the bedroom.

This was one of those ideas that evolved the longer I had been in the house. Originally when I had seen that room in the basement, I thought it might be a quiet little study or office or something like that, I did not originally have the idea of turning it into a bedroom and closet. But in the first day I was in the house, this new idea of the closet and bedroom for that space became a permanent thought process. I had an overwhelming feeling that the new idea was the perfect one for that space. Of all the rooms and possibilities in that house, I knew for sure that this space would be a bedroom with a brand new closet.

It was a huge house and there was so much work to be done. There were quite a few rooms that had odds and ends, things that needed to be taken down, face plates to be removed, light fixtures that needed to be replaced. Some of the rooms had pine paneling which was totally outdated, of course, so we were going through and pulling all of that off the walls. My kids had started working on the kitchen counter tops. They were having a lot of fun demolishing the counter tops in the kitchen. There was a little bit of debris and junk that had been left in the basement, so that was getting hauled out and disposed of. While my kids worked in the kitchen, I decided to get going on that basement room. I knew it was a solid idea, and a good one, so I was eager to get going on that.

The basement room at the bottom of the stairs had tongue and groove pine paneling on the ceiling. It was strange to me that this room would have tongue and groove pine paneling, especially on the ceiling, but it looked like it was done after the original house had been finished. Two of the walls in the room were concrete, but the other two walls were wood framing, and over the framing was some wood paneling that was made of 2x6 boards that fit together with grooves that matched up. These walls appeared to be from when the house was originally built. But the pine tongue and groove paneling for the ceiling seemed like it was an afterthought, done much after the original paneling on the walls. My thought was that the ceiling paneling had been put in along with the other paneling in other parts of the house by the second owner. The second owner was the person I had bought the house from. He probably did the paneling because he liked the nostalgia that paneling brought to a room and he was also probably kind of going for the retro look. But, no matter how retro it looked, it didn't fit in with my vision for the house. So, that had to be taken down before I could strip the wall where I wanted to cut the door in for the closet.

It had been a long day already. The first day, there were people coming and going, thoughts being kicked around and ideas flying, doing a little work here, and doing a little work there. Energies were high and anticipation was thick in the air. It was quite the start to a huge process and it was a big day. That was on a Thursday. We all went home for the day, dirty and tired but still so excited about the prospects this house held for us.

The next day was a Friday and we got an early start. My goal was to have the light demolition work done as soon as possible. This would include removing counter tops, wall paneling and other light things that could be done without a major crew. I wanted to get that all done and get the debris out of there so we could really focus in and concentrate on the more in depth work we were going to do. We were going to have to deal with the electrical wiring, the plumbing and pipes, and the kitchen and bathroom issues that were still at hand. I was there by myself all day long. I had started early, like I said, at about seven in the morning and was there until a little after eleven o'clock that night. This was just a day to do any cleanup that needed to be done and any early stages of demolition that could be complete on a small scale. My kids had come by that day to see how it was going and my family had brought me some lunch for us to share together. We shared our thoughts and ideas while we ate and I talked to them about wanting to cut the wall in the basement. They thought it was a great idea and their encouragement was all I needed. That was it, I was going to do it. And I was going to do it tonight.

As my family was leaving, my son Adam turned to me and he said, "Dad, today is not the only day, you know. Why don't you give it a break and come home? Tomorrow is another day and there are more days after that."

"I know, Adam." I smiled at him, "But I just want to get things done. I want to get as much done as soon as I can so we can be finished."

"I can't wait to see it when it's all finished." Adam replied

"Me too!" I laughed.

My family left and it was just me and the house again. I made sure everything was locked up and I gathered some tools and made sure things were picked up in the kitchen where we had eaten before heading down to the basement. I was eager to get started on that closet for the basement bedroom, I felt tingly and not a bit tired, despite all the work I had already put in that day. I flicked on the light at the top of the stairs and started my descent. How could I have known that in the next few hours I was going to experience one of the biggest moments of my life?

# CHAPTER THREE

I began moving the tools I would need for the project down to the basement. This took several trips as I needed a ladder, light setups and boxes of tools and supplies. I felt like gathering my tools was taking forever. I just had this overwhelming feeling that I needed to hurry. I needed to get it done. That this was a turning moment for me in the house's remodel. I couldn't wait to do it another day, another moment, to get started on that basement room. It had to be done right now. In order to cut the door for the closet, I had to first strip the pine tongue and groove paneling from the room's ceiling. I removed the light fixture from the ceiling and set it aside. Of course, this meant I didn't have the ceiling light to help banish the dark anymore, but I had my light sets so I wasn't worried too much about that. Once I had the light fixture down and out, it took me about 45 minutes or so to get all ceiling paneling removed. Then I had to get my light setups moved and up again. I only had one drop light, so it wasn't the best of lighting, but I figured it was fine for what I was going to do. I was determined to get it done. I felt like if I just did this one piece of the remodel, that all the rest would just fall into place right behind it. Like I was starting with the bottom up and this was the pivotal piece. But beyond my own determination and drive to get this done, there was something else propelling me onward. I thought it was worry starting to set in about the money spent so far on the house itself. But it wasn't worry. I would soon find out what it was, but it wasn't worry.

I got the ceiling paneling down and out of the way and now I wanted to get started on the wall itself. I stood there, looking at the wall where I was going to cut the closet doorway and I'm thinking, 'okay, it's tongue and groove so I need to start at the top of the wall and work my way down toward the floor'. I got up on the ladder and started removing the top row of wood. While I was up on the ladder, I noticed that up near the top of the wall, up against the ceiling, there is tongue and groove paneling that goes both horizontal and vertical. I was perplexed about this and as I was looking at the wall and trying to figure out the best area to start on, I noticed there was a board about three feet long that has a nail at the very top. I hadn't noticed it before because the ceiling panels had been covering it up. The nail was sticking out about half an inch from the board.

I took my hammer and gently loosened up that one nail and started jockeying the board to get it loose. After a few careful minutes of maneuvering the board, that one board lifted out from the tongue and groove below it and I was able to remove it. As I lifted it out, I noticed that the wall behind the board had a cavity that allowed access to the ceiling above the Sheetrock in the hallway. As I examined the framing and Sheetrock in the hall, I noticed that there was a section cut out of the frame and Sheetrock. The cutout was created in such a way that there was an opening above the wall that was about a foot wide and about 8 and one-half or 9 inches tall. The cutout would never have been discovered if I had not removed that one top board. The section of missing wall was entirely hidden by the board I had removed.

I took the boards I had removed and put them in the main basement area with the other boards. Then I got up on the ladder again to inspect the area more. Having no idea why the hole was there, I was a little leery of sticking my hands in there. I didn't know if I would find a dead body or get electrocuted by live and open wires or something even worse. When I got to the top of the ladder, I started to reach in the hole with my hand. Stretching my arm into the hole, I tried to allow light to enter the area, but that was no use. I took a deep breath and shoved my hand in the opening. My hand hit something cold and hard. Surprised, I felt around in the dark, feeling the edges of what I assumed was a piece of tin. Looking up into the wall and knowing what was above where I was perched on the ladder, I assumed I had hit a piece of the ducts and air return from upstairs. I figured it was no big deal.

I got down off the ladder and moved it slightly to a new position. I needed to get more of the boards removed so I could continue my project for the closet cut-in I had planned. I got my ladder repositioned and moved the lights slightly so I could see more of what I was doing up on the ladder. Climbing the ladder once again, my eyes strayed to the hole in the wall once again.

"That's weird." I said to the empty room. "There's writing on it."

The 'tin' I thought was part of the duct system had writing on it and with the new light angle, it didn't look like galvanized metal at all. It looked old and there was writing on the side of the piece I could see. Moving closer to the hole, I reached in and grabbed onto the metal object. I pulled on it and was surprised to feel the metal come loose in my hand. Pulling it carefully from the hole in the wall, I jumped down from the ladder and turned toward the light with my finding. To my great surprise, in my hand I held an old MJB coffee can. The can was slightly rusted in places and had obviously been in its hiding spot a very long time. The plastic lid was still in place, hiding the contents from my view along with a thick layer of dust.

Wiping the dust from the lid with a rag, I started to peel the plastic lid off the can. Having been shut up behind the wall for years, the lid was stuck and I had to pull pretty hard to get the top loose enough to take it off. As I removed the lid from the can, I tilted it toward my work light to get a better look. The inside of the can was dark, but it looked like it was full of trash, wadded up bunches of paper.

"That's weird." I said again, making a habit of talking to myself, "Why is this in there?"

Thinking it was some weird form of early insulation; I carefully put a hand into the can and grabbed a bunch of paper. Pulling it out, my eyes could not believe what I held. Money. It was money crumpled up in there! I knelt down on the drop cloth and dumped the contents of the can onto the floor beside me. There were bunches of bills, paper money, just crammed into this can. There was no rhyme or reason that I could see for the placement of the money. One balled up bill might be a ten dollar bill by itself and another jumble might have a fifty and a twenty crunched up together. I started straightening out the money and looking at it closely. There were hundreds, fifties, and other denominations in the can and it was stuffed full of the bills. One thing I noticed as I sorted and straightened the money from the can was that it was old money. The bills were dated from the 1920s and 1930s. These bills had been in this wall for over fifty years!

My mind was racing, thinking how strange it was to find a can of money inside the wall like that. I put the money carefully back in the can and replaced the lid. I stood there, holding the can, not believing all of it was really happening. Thinking the hole in the wall must be empty now, I climbed back up on the ladder to take a peek in the hole and see how far it goes down. I grabbed one of the clip on lights and took it up the ladder with me. Shining the light into the hole, I craned my neck to look inside the wall. I blinked, letting my eyes adjust to the light suddenly in a dark place. As the light dispelled the gloom, I realized that I was looking at can after can lined up inside the wall.

"Oh my…" my comment drifted off into the air as I stared at what I had found.

I started pulling the cans out and looking inside them. My heart was pounding as I took lid after lid off and found money in each canister. Once I had all of the cans out, there were about nine in all. And each one was stuffed with cash. All of the containers were metal; some of them were like cookie tins, some of them were small fireproof boxes like a homeowner would use to keep documents and papers in. Each one had a lid and was full of money.

Some of the containers were bigger than others. The bigger containers were metal rectangles and square cookie tins. In these large tins, the money was very neatly and tightly stacked like someone had purposely paper clipped it in sections and bundles and then stuffed it into the container. Those larger cans were stuffed so full that they were bulging at the seams and their lids didn't want to stay on. I took all of the cans out and lay them on the drop cloth on the floor. I took off each lid and lined up the cans in a row. Standing above them, I looked down and saw all of that money. Some was crumpled up still, some was neatly put away, but there was a lot of money there and I just stood there and said, "Oh, my God" over and over again.

The wheels in my mind were turning so fast I was afraid I was going to have a short circuit. Just imagine what was racing through my head! This money is all mine, goody, goody! What do I get to buy? Who am I going to give it to? Who can I help with this money? I wonder if it is stolen. Is it really mine? Am I really finding this? Do I get to keep it? Who did it belong to? Why did they put it there? Why are they hiding it? Did anyone else know it was hidden there? Your mind just races, believe me, but it is still the most overwhelming, exciting moment I think I have ever experienced. It was incredible.

I decided to get an idea of how much money was there. I emptied a couple of the cans onto the floor and I was trying to get an idea of how much money it was. I slowly started straightening out the bills and sorting them into piles. All the while I am thinking, 'Wow, the cans that had the money wadded up… they could have as much as maybe three or four thousand dollars in each one. And that's just the small cans.' Doing a quick mental calculation, I figured between the small cans and the larger ones with the organized money in it, there could easily be 20 to 50 thousand dollars in those cans.

"Holy mackerel!" I said, thinking now that I should do something. Should I call someone? Who? What do I do? It's really late by now, close to midnight and who would I call at this hour anyway?

I didn't want to deal with this alone. I ran upstairs and got some large black trash bags. Putting two of the bags together for extra strength, I decided to dump all the contents of the containers into the one double lined bag so I could take it home to deal with it there. I got the bags all ready and started to dump the containers into the bag. As the paper started falling into the bag from the various containers, I noticed that there were also some coins mixed in with the paper money. I dumped one of the large boxes into the bag and noticed some paper falling into the bag that was larger than traditional money. Putting the container down, I rummaged in the bag until I found the large pieces of paper. Pulling them out, I noticed there were several clipped together and they were not bills. They were savings bonds! I put them back in the bag and continued pouring the boxes into the bag. I saw some check stubs go by as well as more savings bonds. I just dumped it all into the bag regardless of what it was. Setting the now full trash bag aside, I looked at the pile of empty containers and wondered what to do with those. I didn't want to just get rid of them or throw them away, but I didn't want to leave them behind either for some reason. I thought about it for a few more moments and then decided to take the containers with me as well. I got a couple more bags and began to put the tins and boxes into those bags. As I'm tossing the tins and boxes into the trash bags, I heard a loud clunk. Pausing, I wondered what that could have been. I thought I had emptied all the cans into the bags, but there was obviously something I had missed.

I started taking the cans back out of the bag one by one and shaking it to see which one had rattled. Finally, I found the offender and opened the lid to see what was inside. I tipped the can over onto my hand and felt something heavy drop onto my palm. Lifting the can up, I saw that there was a small block of wood in the palm of my hand. It had weird carvings all over it and I turned it over and over, trying to figure out what it was. It was kind of heavy, but it was a real hard wood, a solid piece of wood. I figured it was heavy because it was wood. Maybe it didn't weigh any more than itself, so I thought it was kind of odd to find a block of wood in with all this money. I didn't see any hinges or pulleys on the block, so I figured it was a keepsake and tossed it back in the can. I picked up the bags and set them in the basement by the base of the stairs.

Heading back into the small bedroom, I looked at the wall. I could not believe what had just happened. I came in here wanting to cut in a closet and was leaving having found thousands of dollars hidden in the wall. It was like something out of a mystery novel! I decided to cover the hole up. I climbed up the ladder, took one last peek inside the wall (just in case, you know) and began putting the board back up just the way I had found it. I sealed it back up, put my tools and lights away and headed out into the basement. As I grabbed the bags and headed upstairs, I suddenly felt like someone was watching me. I turned quickly and looked into the dark of the basement. There didn't seem to be anyone there. I stood for a minute or so, looking around the basement and wondering how the money had got inside the wall and who had put it there.

I went upstairs and dropped the bags in the kitchen while I went through the house locking up. On my way out, I grabbed the bags and lugged them out to my car. I threw the bags into the trunk of my car and got in, ready to head home.

On the way home I called my wife to tell her about what I'd found.

"Sarah, you're not going to believe what happened." I told her as soon as she picked up.

"Are you alright?" Hearing the tension in my voice, she had become alarmed.

"Yes, I'm fine, but something happened."

"What? What happened?" She hated it when I kept her in suspense. So I let her wait a moment more before telling her.

"I was in the basement, you know, in that little room where I wanted to cut in the closet?"

"Yes. Ok."

" Well, I was up on the ladder, and I started pulling boards down so I could cut into the wall behind that paneling down there…"

"Did you fall?" She was impatient to get to the heart of the matter.

"No," I said, indignant. I was a professional! "I didn't fall, Sarah."

"Then what?!"

"Well, as I was saying," I continued, dragging it out, "I pulled off the top board and there was like a hole or something behind it."

"A hole?"

"Yeah, a hole. In the wall. There was a hole in the wall and so I looked inside there and there was a can."

"There was a can in the wall?"

"Yes," I sighed, "let me finish."

"Well hurry up!"

"Fine, there was a can in the wall and it had money it in." I said in a rush.

"Money?"

"Yes, money. Bunches of wadded up money, in the can."

"Really?" She was sounding excited now and I began to feel excited again too.

"Yeah, lots of it. Old money too, like from the 1920s or something. And then, when I got back up on the ladder, I saw there were more cans in the hole in the wall."

"What?!"

"Yes, there were like nine cans in there, all full of money and savings bonds and stuff."

"Oh my god," Sarah said. "Oh my god!"

"I know!" I was grinning and I could hear the smile in her voice as we talked.

I glanced at the clock on the dash of my car and saw it was past midnight but I didn't care. I asked Sarah to get a big sheet and put it on the bed because I was bringing home the money and we were going to dump it out on the bed. We talked a little more, both very excited about the treasure trove I had found. We both didn't really know what to say about it, didn't know what we should do. But we did know that very shortly, our bed was going to have tons of cash spilled out on it.

It took me about 20 minutes to get to my house. I grabbed the bag of money, leaving the other two bags in the trunk of my car and packed the bag upstairs. Sarah met me at the door and followed me upstairs without a word. I upended the bag over the center of our bed and we both stood there silently looking at it. There was quite a lot of money there. Some was still wadded up money and some was stacked and folded while other items were clipped together. There were a few coins and other paper items like savings bonds and check stubs as well as what appeared to be actual checks. Altogether, it was a sizable heap. Sarah and I looked at one another and grinned. Without a word being spoken between us, we sat on opposite sides of the bed and proceeded to straighten out and sort all the money. We put the savings bonds in a pile and the coins in another pile, but all the bills got sorted, straightened and organized.

After Sarah and I had sorted all the money out, I went down to the garage to get some storage tubs I had purchased for organizing our garage shelves. The tubs were made of see through plastic and they were about 14 inches wide, 20 inches deep and about 15 inches tall. I brought up six or seven of those tubs to the bedroom, and we put the money into separate bins. When we were finished, we had about two and a half tubs of 20 dollar bills, an overflowing tub of 50 dollar bills, a very full tub of 100 dollar bills, and stacks of miscellaneous items such as 1,000 dollar bills, savings bonds and special currency. The special currency items were things from banks that no longer existed like the Bank of Astoria and the Bank of Oregon City. Those special currency items were odd sized, larger than the bills we are used to these days and were dated from the late 1800s. The coins that we gathered together from the haul were gold Indian head coins as well as a few miscellaneous silver coins. I had never really paid attention to currency. It was just something that sifted through my fingers so fast that I didn't pay any attention to it. I knew it had numbers on it, but that was about it. As we finished packaging the money up into the bins, we had currency from the late 1800s as late as the mid-1970s.

It had taken us about four hours to organize the money. During that four hours my mind was going crazy. I thought of so many things like: 'What can I buy?', 'What am I going to do with it?', 'I can pay for my kids' college!', 'I can pay off our debt!', and 'We are not going to have to worry about money!' The thought that finally struck me was, 'I am not going to have to worry about this house selling for enough money because we are going to be fine!'. Then my thoughts turned towards other related topics such as, 'Who did it belong to?' and 'Do we have to give it back?' I wondered over and over if I should be doing something with the money, if it didn't really belong to me and if I would have to give it to someone else and not get to keep it for myself and my family.

# PART TWO: THE HOUSE

EILEEN MAKI

# CHAPTER FOUR

As the reality of finding the money began to sink it, I realized there were issues to be dealt with here that I would never have thought of if this hadn't happened to me. I began to think of the legal, spiritual and moral aspects of finding someone else's money. It monopolized my thoughts day and night. What is the right thing to do? Regardless of what I wanted to do, what was the right thing? I can easily tell you exactly what I wanted to do; I wanted to keep that money and use it for myself and my family. I think anyone would agree with a find like that, that's the first thing you think of. How you can spend it, invest it or use it to make your life better and the life of those you love. Your first instinct is, 'I want to keep it, it's mine'. But as you will find in the pages that follow, the decision was far more involved than just my wants and the needs of my family.

I didn't know what to do with all that money and the weight of the decision was heavy on my heart and mind. I decided I needed an unbiased third party to help me with this decision. Maybe they would think of something I hadn't and I definitely needed to know what the law was. What was I legally responsible to do? I thought and thought about who I could talk to, who I could trust and who would be the biggest help to me in this situation.

Finally, I contacted a close family friend and talked at length with them about what had happened. I explained how it happened, where it happened, and what all it involved. This family friend listened, asked some questions and then advised me to get legal counsel. Deciding this was a good idea, I did some research and called someone to get an opinion. This was someone I had never dealt with before or talked to before. It was kind of weird to me to be talking about personal information and details of my life with a perfect stranger. I guess people do it all the time, but it was foreign to me. So the process of securing legal counsel was kind of an interesting process to go through. When I located what I thought was a respectable and reliable counsel, I called and explained who I was, why I was calling and what I had experienced. After discussing the issue for some time and giving this stranger all the pertinent details, his advice was to reenact the sequence of events that took place, take pictures and make an account of the exact actions that had taken place.

The very next day, after talking with my legal counsel, I went to the house. It felt weird walking in there, like the whole place was somehow different for me this time. I found myself wondering if there were things in the other walls in different parts of the house. I shook my head and concentrated on the task at hand. I had taken the containers back to the house for the purpose of taking pictures. I took pictures of the containers, the opening in the wall and the boards that concealed the hole. I went through the process again, exactly as I remembered it. I took the first board off and then exposed the containers. Then, container by container I documented how I had found them, how they were placed in the storage area above the hallway. I even took a picture of the little wood block I had found that had carvings on it.

I was a pretty strong Christian. The more facets that were exposed in this situation, the more I began to think and pray on what the right thing was to do. I knew in my heart of hearts that I wanted to do what was right. Even if it went against what I wanted to do, I knew I had to do what was right. But what was morally right and spiritually correct in this situation? I didn't even know for sure who this all belonged to! So I prayed about it and consulted my legal counsel. The legalities dealt with facts and case history and the fact of the matter was that there was no case history to apply in my particular situation. The problem was people who find themselves in this type of situation did not often go telling someone about it to find out what the right thing to do was. They probably just kept the money and didn't think twice about it. A lot of people just didn't share this kind of information. It is not generally discussed, and if it is, it doesn't end up in the court system because the few court cases that were researched didn't specifically pertain to these circumstances, which was interesting.

While the dilemma of what to do with the money stewed in the back of my mind, I had to do something with it. I did not feel comfortable leaving that kind of money and wealth laying around my house, so I needed somewhere to put it. I figured a safe deposit box was the best way to go and called my bank to get the details. All the branches close to my home did not have a box available at all. Finally, I called the branch close to my work and they had one, and only one, available. The box they had was 12 by 12 by 24. It was the only one they had and it was their biggest box. I knew all of the treasure trove wouldn't fit in that box, so I took the largest denomination currency and put it all in a briefcase. I went to the bank, filled out all the forms and was shown to the safety deposit box room where I began putting the money carefully into the box. I wanted to fit as much of the currency in the box as possible. The safe deposit box was full when I was done. You would have been lucky to put even a small paper clip in the box when I was done putting the money in there! I had packed the money carefully and snuggly in the box.

With the money secure, I continued the process of remodeling the house. We still had several months to go before we would be ready to sell and I was busy scheduling work, doing work myself and trying to figure out what to do with the money. In addition, I was still working my regular, full-time job.

I still had the specialty money at home and I wanted to find out what it was worth and keep it protected from damage. I went to an office supply store and I bought some acrylic money pouches. You know, the ones that currency is placed into when it is collectible? So I got one pouch for each year in each denomination. I put the currencies in the pouches and then in a zip-up binder for storage and safekeeping.

Over the next few weeks, I spent several hours researching the currency on-line and talking to currency brokers. I met with people in the money circles and found out some interesting information about currency collecting and trading. I found out that those circles deal strictly in cash and there is not really much of a record. They typically pay you 80 percent of the market value right up front in cash, and a lot of collectors, for whatever reason, don't really keep records. So you show up to a market with 100,000 dollars in old bills and they give you 100,000 dollars in new bills and you walk out the door. That's it, that's the end of the transaction. There is no record, traceable or otherwise. I found that to be interesting. Interesting, and scary. I also began to understand why the courts didn't have a record of this type of situation. If you could take the old money and exchange it for new money and there was no record of it, what would stop someone from doing just that and keeping the money for themselves?

We had counted the money the night I had brought it home from the wall, and I knew the face value of the currency to be in the neighborhood of 245,000 dollars. After my initial research on values of collectible currency, I estimated the market value of all of it (including the oddball currency that you couldn't put a value on) to be around 325,000 dollars. That was my initial calculation. I would find out later that it was worth much more than that, in more ways than one.

In with the odd documents, there were other papers mixed in. There were checks that were written out to the original homeowner. When I had purchased the house, I got a short history on it. The man who had built the house was an elderly man when he passed away. In that house, he had raised two daughters and outlived his wife. His name was Harold Bell.

Harold had owned a local business that dealt mostly in cash, and it is my belief that because he was raised during the depression he didn't put any trust in banks. I began to form an explanation for the money being in the wall as I had found it. I believed that Harold, because he didn't believe in banks and because he dealt in cash, would bring cash home on a daily basis. I could picture him stuffing it into a container, and when that container was full, he would go down in the basement and he would put it in the hole in the wall. He would then start a new container, and he proceeded to do that over a period of a number of years. After going through the dated papers and money over and over, it began to be my belief that it had been approximately 14 years from the date I found it since someone had placed anything in those containers.

Harold had died about five years prior to me buying the house. That means there would have been 9 years that he lived in the house and he didn't touch, add to, or take anything out of those containers in any way. He was in his mid 90s when he passed away, so that meant that he would have stopped messing with the stored treasure when he was in his mid-80s. As I mentioned, I knew that Harold had raised two daughters and outlived his wife. I did some research on the daughters and found that they were still living in the area and his wife had indeed passed away about 6 years before he had. Harold had lived alone in the house for about 6 years before he passed away. So there the money sat, gathering dust and value, until I stumbled onto it in my efforts to cut in a closet in the basement bedroom.

One of the really odd things about what actually transpired in the process of remodeling the house is that I never did end up cutting that hole in the wall to put a closet in that basement bedroom. I was so driven, so emphatic about putting in that closet down there. It was the project I wanted to start first, the piece I felt driven to complete before anything else. The unused space in the hallway ended up being added to the room on the other side of the hallway, not being used for a closet. The plan I had felt so strongly about to begin with sort of fizzled and died once I had found the money in the wall. I often pondered this turn of events and wondered why I had felt so compelled to complete that portion of the remodel and later abandoned it altogether. But as my story progresses, you will understand what transpired, as I do now. Had I never had the compulsion to put in that closet, the money would have gone undiscovered, just as it had for the person who owned the house before me.

Once the money was found and safely away, I continued the remodel without acting on the hoard I had found. I let it sit and let my thoughts stew. After all, I still had a house to sell before I spent too much more time and money on the thing. This was, at the end of it, a business investment that needed to be completed and followed through on. And boy did I follow through on it!

# CHAPTER FIVE

While continuing to perform the remodel, we ran into a few problems. We ran into plumbing and electrical problems. We ran into dry rot problems. We ran into pest problems. It was just like being on one of those TV shows where everything that can go wrong does and it's great entertainment. Only this was not very entertaining when you were the one going through it. Because I had forgone the inspection, I had bought a house and had no idea what was there until we started the real in depth work of remodeling. When we started digging around and tearing things down, we started to find things we wished we had never found. The budget continued to grow, growing almost double what we had initially budgeted for, which tapped out all of my resources. I was using credit cards that I didn't even know I had, because the money that I had found, it really wasn't mine yet and I didn't know at this point if it ever would be. So none of the money that was found was touched whatsoever for any reason until we could determine who it belonged to and what the proper course of action was.

As time allowed, I went through the miscellaneous papers that were found in with the money. Some of the newer money was mixed in with documents containing names of Harold and his daughters, so I knew my original theory of who had put the money there had to be true. It was Harold. There were checks in with the money payable to Harold Bell. The checks were from different individuals for varying and small amounts. The amounts of the checks ranged anywhere from 10 to 25 dollars. There were several of those in the can. Knowing that Harold had dealt mostly with cash only, I figured he had received checks from people whom he knew were low on funds or needed a little help and so he just put their checks in his cans and never cashed them. That way, his customer could feel like they had paid him for their goods, but he could also give them a little help without them losing any pride over it.

There were also the savings bonds that I had mentioned before. There was one savings bond in each of his daughter's names. Some for Rose and some for Karen. There was a paycheck stub with Harold's name on it in the mix from Social Security. There were some other miscellaneous and insignificant pieces of paperwork in there, which specifically identified him as the individual who placed it there. I wondered why those random pieces of paper were in there. I noticed that the miscellaneous papers seemed to be mixed in with the newer currency, so I thought maybe that's the time Harold started going downhill with his health and so he was putting things in the can that didn't make much sense. On the other hand, maybe there was a hidden meaning that I didn't understand.

After a few weeks, my legal counsel called me and said they had found some information that they felt would answer the question of legal ownership for the funds beyond a doubt. At the next opportunity I had, I went down to their office to find out the news. Having never been to his office before, only spoken to him on the phone, I was pleased with their offices. They were muted and tasteful in design as a legal office most often appears. Things were clean, magazines were new and the receptionist was welcoming. I sat on the green couches and waited my turn. Finally, my counsel called me in and I was ready to hear the news.

"Larry," he said, extending his and to shake mine. "David Brand. It's a pleasure to meet you and I'm so glad you brought this most interesting matter to me."

David was tall and distinguished with dark hair that was graying at his temples. He had a warm smile that didn't quite touch his eyes but I believed it anyway. He motioned to a chair across from his desk and I took a seat.

"Thanks." I said. Not knowing what else to say and wanting to get to the bottom of the matter at hand.

"I'm sure you are eager to hear of what I've learned, Larry, so I'll get right to the point."

It was as if he had read my mind!

"It took quite a bit of digging and analyzing your particular situation. However, we believe that this case is unique in that you can identify who the items belong to."

Mr. Brand went on to explain that there are a variety of different 'found' properties. There was mislaid property, treasure trove property and many others along with descriptions and legal definitions of what the type of property would entail. What made my case so different was that we, rather than just finding money, had also found the documents that more likely than not identified Harold as the individual who had put the money and other items into the hiding place. Because the owner of the property could be identified, that made the property fit the category of 'lost, hidden, or mislaid property'. Lost, hidden or mislaid property belongs to the original individual unless that individual is no longer living. In the case that the original owner was no longer living (as Harold was not), it belonged then, to the rightful heirs of the original owner (Karen and Rose). It did not matter who found it or where the original owner placed the property. And it did not matter who owned the real estate that the property was found in or on. Because the owner could most likely be identified, then legally I was told and advised that it belonged to that individual and/or the rightful heirs. Having already conducted that research, I knew Harold and his wife, Esther, to be passed on. I also knew that both of Harold's daughters, Rose and Karen, were still living and that they were his rightful heirs. Hearing this new information made the situation and the decision an easy one for me.

The moral aspect for me had been 'Whose money was it?' And once I had determined that, then that is who the money belonged to. It made sense to me and seemed fair once you thought about it. I mean, if you turn the tables around and if my dad had placed money in his home and then someone else found it, I don't believe they would have a right to it. It was his money and so therefore it would rightfully be mine. End of story. So I knew I had to do the same. It was a matter of answering that question. I had already determined that I really couldn't keep it, but I wanted to be certain, and legally I was informed that was the case. Once I heard the legalities of the situation, it was pretty cut and dry for me that the money needed to go back to the two daughters.

Now the question was, how did I go about giving the money back to them? What was the process involved? I wanted to wait until the house was done. I wanted to do some research and find out a little bit more about whom the girls were and what their situations were. There was a lot involved there, and so I wasn't in any rush. When I was preparing to leave my attorney's office, David gave me a final piece of information.

"You know, Larry," he started as he stood up to walk me to the door, "because of client privilege confidentiality, we cannot tell you what to do with it. We can just tell you what we found legally, but we can't tell anybody about it, so you can do whatever you want to do with it."

I looked at him and he smiled as he shook my hand.

"Most people that I have dealt with or most situations like this, the individual who found the money would just keep it to themselves and not tell anybody, especially this sizable of an amount."

I shook his hand and left the building with all of the information swimming around in my head. I sat in my car for a while before I started the engine to leave.

The temptation to keep everything was very strong. After all I had recently gone through to get started in my new house remodeling business only to have to go into debt again to finish the house, then finding the money that could make it all worthwhile. It was almost more than I could process. Then I thought about the money that currency collecting people run in cash circles with no receipts, I could have easily taken that. I could easily have gone to the next currency market and cashed it all in for the 250,000 dollars and ended up with common current currency that would be untraceable. Don't think the temptation wasn't there. It was always there, needling me, egging me on to just keep the money. No one would know, they didn't have to know. But it just wasn't the right thing to do, and there was a lot involved. I thought about my religious beliefs, my moral beliefs, and my children. What lesson did I want my children to learn from this experience? Did I want them to be greedy and keep things for themselves that did not really belong to them? I had not shared all of the information with my children at this point, but as we move forward, I will explain that process and their involvement and what transpired on that front.

All being said and done to this point, a decision on the horizon, I was left with two thoughts that nagged at me; Rose and Karen. I had done some preliminary research to learn their names and confirm that the names on the security bonds were those of Harold's daughters. I determined they were both still living and verified that fact. In the process, I also found out that both daughters had been married and also had children of their own. They were both still married, lived near one another and they were very close to each other emotionally as well.

Surprisingly enough, both Rose and Karen stopped by the house during the next couple of months of remodeling. Each of them stopped by the house completely of their own accord and on separate occasions to introduce themselves to me and to see the house. They spent time telling me about how much they appreciated the changes to the house. They spent some time chatting with me and talking about their father, Harold. Their stories explained their father to me and what kind of a man he had been.

The girls talked of a man who was very strict in his ways. He was very old fashioned and extremely strong willed. He was all about money. He was always busy and he worked every day of his life at the local business he owned. He was a proud and productive man and when his driver's license was taken away, he pretty much gave up on life. He had told his oldest daughter, Karen that if he couldn't work then life was not worth living. From the point he lost his driver's license to the years immediately following, he basically gave up. After that, it wasn't too long before he passed. This explained a lot and confirmed what I had thought about Harold not using the cans in the wall the last few years of his life. He had given up, was ready to join his wife in the afterlife that awaited him.

He was very proud of his home, but he didn't like change. His family would always suggest updates and renovations for the house but he was very adamant about the fact that he had done a perfect job building the house. He said it was the best built house in town and it didn't need any changes. He had done everything right the first time and that's exactly why he had done it the way he had, so it would be perfect. And it was. He didn't want anything to do with change. The daughters were both very clear of the fact that although they loved the updates and remodeling efforts for their old home, Harold would not be pleased with all the changes we were making if he had still been alive.

During a rare time when both Rose and Karen were at the house talking to me, we were standing in the kitchen when I set the stage for the later delivery. I wanted to wait until the house was finished.

"When the house is finished, ladies," I told them, "I want you to come back and have a look around before I sell it."

"Oh!" They both exclaimed, "That would be lovely, Mr. Campbell." Rose declared.

"Please, call me Larry." I said and smiled.

"Alright, Larry. We look forward to it then!" Karen said as they left the house.

I walked them out to their car and hoped the remodeling wouldn't take too much longer so I could give them the inheritance they deserved with good faith and a happy heart. My intent was to have them both there at the same time so I could tell them about the money and tell them about what their father had left for them. During the next few weeks and months that followed, the remodel continued to gain steam. I was glad I had gotten to meet the daughters, because I knew without a doubt what the right path would be and my conscious was clear. As soon as the remodel was done, I would have the sisters back and they would be rewarded handsomely for their wait.

# CHAPTER SIX

As the remodeling efforts continued, a lot of weird events began to take place. People who frequented the house told me of things happening in the house that were odd or mysterious. Subcontractors who were hired for various jobs would report to me that their tools and equipment had been moved overnight when no one was in the house. Noises were heard and when someone went to investigate, the noise stopped suddenly. As the work went on, it seemed like everyone who came into contact with the house experienced something weird. Everyone that is, except me. I did not experience any of these happenings for myself. However, as time went on, I began to experience events that were very specific to me and what I had gone through with the house so far. At the time I was experiencing the events, it was a mystery, but as events unfolded it became more and more clear how and why these things happened.

One of the things I did experience, however, happened shortly after the money was found. As the work for remodeling the house continued, I needed and hired some framers to work in the basement. In preparation for the framers to begin their work, I needed to continue to do some light demolition work that was required. I also did other things that required me to be in the basement such as hauling lumber to the basement and cleaning up. On one particular evening, I was there until after midnight sweeping the basement floor and cleaning up to be sure it was ready for the framers to begin their work the next day. The basement was spotless when I was finished. I picked up all the debris and everything was swept clean and put away.

The next morning I got to the house early, at about 6 a.m., because I wanted to be sure that everything was ready for the framers. My family and I had affectionately named the room where I found the money, the

'Treasure Room'. I walked through the basement, making sure all was ready for the workers that would be there later, and right in the middle of the treasury room was a piece of paper, money. I stopped in the doorway of the room, not sure I was seeing what I was seeing. But there it was, smack dab in the middle of the room, on the floor all by itself was the bill. I went into the room and picked it up. Turning it over for inspection, I could see it was an old 100 dollar bill. I was dated 1925. I put the bill in my pocket and examined the room. There was no explanation of how it got there. I checked the rafters, the board on the wall, the floor, I checked everywhere. There was absolutely no explanation as to how or why the bill had got there. I took the bill with me and added it to the rest of the money at my house.

Another experience I had in the house was when I was in the process of redoing the upstairs bathroom. I was doing some demolition in order to take out the old bathtub that was in there. I had to break the tub into big sections with a sledge hammer so I could take it out of the bathroom. As I was hauling pieces of the tub out, I saw some paper out of the corner of my eye. Underneath the rubble of the bathtub, there was a piece of paper sticking out just a bit from the messy hole in the floor I had just made. I began to clear away the dust from the demolition of the tub and the powder from the old grout in order to get under the floor where the tub had sat, sealed by grout and tile for years. As I cleared the debris away, I couldn't believe what I was seeing. It was a bill, it was currency. I picked it out of the mess and discovered it was a 50 dollar bill. Like the 100 dollar bill I had found, it was dated 1925. I was puzzled as to how the money had got there. I looked around in the hole in the floor, but this was the only one I found. How did it get under there? That part of the floor had been sealed underneath the bathtub for many years. It just didn't make any sense. I took that bill home with me also and added it to the other money.

A third incident occurred when I was working in the basement again. Once again, it was late and I was doing some framing in the Treasure Room. I was on the floor in that room, with work lights up. I was the only one in the house as the other workers and my family had gone home hours before. I saw a movement out of the corner of my eye and turned my head slightly to see what it was. To my astonishment, I saw an older man walk by the doorway in the hallway. I didn't recognize him as anyone I knew, so I jumped up and ran over to the doorway to have a look. I had been using an air compressor, so I had ear protection on and hadn't heard a thing. I quickly unplugged the compressor, threw my ear protectors on the floor and ran out to the main basement area shouting.

"Who's there? Who's there? I saw you, I know you're here!"

I ran through the entire basement and found nothing. Stopping in the main basement area again, I paused to listen and look around without moving. I saw and heard nothing.

I went upstairs, thinking the person had run up the stairs when I had seen them and came running and shouting at them. I went through every room and everything was locked. Every door, every window. Nothing was out of place and nothing was touched. There was never anybody in that house except me. Me and whatever it is I saw walk by the door in the basement.

From that point on, I always felt like I was being watched when I was in the house. Especially when I was in the house alone. I had felt like I was not alone before on several nights when working in the house by myself, but I had always chalked it up to the 'Boogie Man' or just being nervous about being at the house alone in the dead of the night. I never really paid any attention to it. Now, I acknowledged it and recognized the feeling. It was not a sinister feeling, like I was in danger or being threatened. It was not a negative feeling at all. I fell in love with the house and every time I went to the house, I felt at home, like I belonged there. Spectral Peeping Tom or not, I never felt uncomfortable in the house or that I was not wanted there. Although I never felt poorly, you could always feel the presence of something or someone in the house when you knew you were the only one there. As I spent more and more time in the house, I began to get the feeling even when others were there. I began to recognize that the feeling of being watched was very different than the feeling you get when you know a human being is in the room with you and may be watching what you're doing. It was not the same feeling at all. I asked other people too, and they said the same thing. So I wasn't the only one to feel the presence in the house. I had a friend of mine come over and help me do some work at the house. As we were working in the basement, I began to feel the presence. Being used to it at this point, I said nothing, knowing my friend would think I had lost my mind if I discussed such things with him. We had been there a few hours, working side by side when he surprised me.

"Hey Larry." He began. I looked over at him. He was a few feet from where I was and we were working on the floor in the basement together.

"Yeah?" I answered.

"Do you feel like there's someone watching us?" He glanced around as if he expected someone to pounce on him from behind. He looked kind of spooked.

"Yeah." I said. "I get that feeling a lot in this house."

"Oh," he looked relieved, "must be because it's so big."

"Yeah, must be."

Neither one of us said anything else about it, but it was nice to have someone validate the feeling who hadn't been working in the house as much as me and wasn't prone to those types of feelings any more than I was.

As the remodel progressed, I had an inspection coming up and I needed to have some electrical work done as soon as possible. I did some networking and through a really good friend of mine, I found an electrician that came highly recommended. He was willing to do my job on the side during evenings and weekends. He had been doing remodeling for years and he was just an excellent find for my needs. I gave him a call and set it up so that he was going to come in on a Tuesday, Wednesday, Thursday, Friday evening after his normal job and then finish it Saturday and Sunday. The inspection was on the following Monday, so I was cutting it close. I knew this guy came with excellent references and was really good at what he did, so I wasn't worried about the work being done before the deadline for the Monday inspection.

I actually called and made sure the inspection was scheduled for that Monday. That is how sure we were that we were going to have all the work done on that day that needed to be completed for the inspection. I didn't give the electrician any money up front. We didn't sign any paperwork or draw up any work contracts. We just had a verbal agreement and a handshake to seal the deal. My new electrician went out and bought lighting equipment, accessories, wiring, everything he needed to do the job. He brought it all into the house and set up what he needed in the basement, leaving the remaining supplies and tools in the garage. He brought in his ladder, his tools, and he started installing the electrical wiring that was needed. He came as agreed on Tuesday, Wednesday and Thursday evenings. In fact, he was there on Thursday night when I left. I left late that night, which was common for me, telling him goodnight as I passed the room he was working in.

"How's it going?" I asked, pausing in the doorway.

"Just fine, Larry. Everything is going according to plan."

"So we are on schedule for the inspection on Monday, then?"

"Oh absolutely. No problem."

"Great." I said. Everything was falling into place. "I'm headed home."

"Alright," he said from his position on the ladder.

"You're the last one here, so please lock up when you're through."

"You bet," he said and gave a little wave as I turned to leave.

I had no reason at that time to think that he would not be back. I was unable to get over there again until Saturday but expected the electrical work to be done. During the week he had been working at the house I never knew him to leave tools or equipment out. Whenever I had been there in the morning after he had been there the night before, the next morning his tools were put away, the lights were shut off, the ladder was set down and you wouldn't have known he had been there working. That's how clean he left it. On this particular Saturday, I went into the house and heard faint music playing. I should have been the only one in the house, so

I followed the sound to see where it was coming from. The music led me to the room my electrician had been working in on Thursday when I had told him goodnight. I was puzzled when I looked around and it looked like there was very little work done in the room. The music was coming from a small radio on the windowsill. His ladder was still up and his tools were still out with materials spread out on the floor ready for use. It was as if the electrician had left on Thursday, right after we had talked and he hadn't been back since.

Concerned that something had happened to him, I called and left a message for him on his cell phone on Saturday morning. That was the only number I had for him. On Saturday afternoon I still hadn't heard from him and I was getting worried. I got a hold of my friend that had referred him to me.

"His stuff is still there?" My friend asked me over the phone when I called him.

"Yeah," I said, standing in the room where the evidence still sat. "It's all here. He left the radio on, his tools out, the ladder up. It's all just sitting here like he went to the bathroom and never came back or something."

"I've worked with him for years, Larry, and that's just not like him. I wouldn't worry about it. If he said he'll have it done on Sunday, he'll have it done on Sunday."

"Ok." I said and hung up.

Sunday came and went with no word from the electrician.

On Monday I had to call and cancel the inspection. I also had to call around and find another electrician to come in and finish the work. I took everything that the old electrician had left, the leftover materials, his tools and everything, and I put it aside in the garage for him. The new electrician bought all new materials, brought in his own stuff, re-did quite a bit of what the other electrician had done and continued to finish the work as normal. To this day, I still have never heard back from the first electrician, which is just not his character at all from what I understand. I did some checking and found out that he was alive and well and still doing electrical work. But I could not get him to return my phone calls or tell me what happened. He never came to retrieve his materials and tools either.

I remember thinking it was very strange and wondering what happened to the man. I sent him a letter even, asking him to call me and we could set up a time so he could get his tools and materials back. I never received a response from that letter either. As I would find out much later, he had good reason to do what he had done.

# CHAPTER SEVEN

At long last, the remodel on the house was finished. As we prepared to put the house on the market and sell it off, the area experienced downpours of monsoon proportions. It was four days and four nights straight of torrential rains. Record flooding was being reported all over the place and it reminded me of the flood we had about twenty years prior in the area as well. I had been to check on the house on a Thursday night and everything was fine. On Saturday morning, we received a call from the Realtor that we might have an offer coming in and the potential new buyer wanted to meet with the Realtor at the house on Sunday to have a look around.

My Realtor, I was still using Sam, went over to the house early on Sunday morning to do the magic that Realtors do. He planned to turn the lights on, put some mood music on and just kind of make sure everything was in order. Going down the basement steps to prepare the basement for viewing, as soon as he stepped off the bottom step into the main basement area, he stepped into 4 inches of water. The entire basement had 4 to 6 inches of water all through it. Sam called me and I raced over there.

After some initial investigation, I discovered what had happened. The storm drain on the back of the house that carried the entire watershed from the roof had become plugged. This caused the water draining from the roof to become backed up into a window well that was adjacent to the storm drain. The window well had a window in it that went directly into the Treasure Room. The window was about 3 feet wide and about 2 feet tall, but it was about 4 feet below grade level. The water from the rains and the roof downpour was pooling in the backyard and then running into the window well which was completely submerged under water. In short, the Treasure Room window in the basement was under about 4 feet of water, causing the water to continuously seep in around the opening of the window and into the basement. Apparently, the water had been oozing in around the window for about 2 or 3 days now.

I set to work and was able to reroute the storm drain and pump out the water from the basement to prevent any further damage. We pulled the carpets up and got air handlers in there that were able to dry out the basement using dehumidifiers. Thankfully, we were able to get everything dried out. Because the water had been standing from a few inches to about six inches for several days, we had to cut the sheet rock back 4 feet up on the walls. We also removed the insulation and then put mildew retardant on everything, including inside those walls. After all the treatments had dried, we put in new insulation, new Sheetrock, mud, tape and texture, new paint and new moldings. We were lucky to be able to get it all back together without too much terrible damage. We also lucked out on the carpets and were able to reuse it. We got the carpets out and dried in just the nick of time to allow us to reuse it and not have to purchase all new carpeting for the basement. After the damage had been repaired, we located the offending downspout and proceeded to put in a new storm drain. Once everything had been taken care of, we had to document all of the damage and repairs for the house disclosures. I wrote it all up and included before and after pictures of the area that had flooded. On top of that, we had to get a mildew expert in the basement so they could give a rating on the moisture content level. Then, we had to include the mildew expert's report in the house disclosures as well. Everyone who looked at the house from that point on had to have the damage and repairs explained; what the extent of the damage was from the flooding and what had been done to repair it. This was a huge turnoff to a lot of people.

So there we were. We still had a big house with a big disclosure statement that wasn't selling. The economy was getting worse and the state economists were predicting a double dip recession. To make matters even worse, the housing market was going down the drain faster than everything else was. At first, thinking we would save money on Realtor fees, we tried selling the house ourselves. We had tons of people come through and were hopeful that it would sell without a lot more effort on our part. The response we had was nothing short of incredible, but we were getting absolutely no offers on the house at all. Even when we listed the house with the offending disclosure statements, we still got a huge turnout of people looking at the house. There were literally record numbers of people coming through the house. Even though we were selling without a Realtor at that time, Sam would bring his brokers in just so they could see the amount of people flowing through the house. Because they had never really seen that many people going through one house before. It was like nothing any of them had ever seen before. We had people coming back 3, 4 and 5 times to look through, make notes, ask questions and call their friends, neighbors, relatives and whoever else they wanted to talk to about the house. Everybody that went through it loved the house. They raved about the remodel features I had painstakingly done and overseen. They loved the basement, the kitchen, the redone bathrooms and all other parts of the beautiful house, but still, no one was making any offers.

We had been through so much with this house. It was amazing when you stopped to think about what all had happened in the short time since we'd bought it. The remodeling project itself grew from the originally budgeted amount of 65,000 dollars, to just a little over 115,000 dollars by the time it was all said and done. I had never imagined that this project would cost that much. The additional expenses hugely chunked away at my estimated profits from the eventual sale of the house. In addition to the unexpected budget expenses plus the repairs to the basement. We went through the flood, the stress of the remodel and the stress of the tanking housing market. We had the stress of the house not selling, the stress of the flood and the stress of finding the money and that whole situation still hanging over our heads. Last but not least, we had the pressure of the time constraint. Every month that the house sat unsold on the market, was another month that we had to pay 4,500 dollars for the mortgage payment. We were going to be taking a huge loss on the house very soon, no matter how much it sold for. That is, if it sold at all.

So there we sat; the highs and the lows of the entire experience all laid out before us. We had achieved closure with most of the issues that had come up; deciding what to do with the money, remodeling the house, the issues with the flooding and the other repairs. Now we had a house that was in pristine condition sitting on the market with tons of people going through it and nobody buying it. This continued to go on for week after week. And each week that passed that we didn't even get an offer on the house, was another week that I wondered if I had done the right thing. I was working two jobs, more like three and a half with the house being a job and a half all on its own. I was tired and so far, had spent upwards of about five months on this house. We had purchased the house in July, and the project had now spanned the months of July, August, September, October, and now was heading into November before we put it on the market. Because of the flood, I had to take it off the market while we made repairs and got everything inspected again. After the disclosures were ready, I wasn't able to get the house back on the market again until just before the holidays in December. So now we were in the dead of winter, and I was begrudged to admit that I was becoming more and more discouraged by the day. Here I had the biggest discovery of my life and possibly the most momentous event in the history of my life and the life of the others involved, and I'm in a situation that just doesn't seem to have any hope in sight. It was such a roller coaster of ups and downs. I have to admit that it was a pretty tough time to go through. I wasn't the only one discouraged, either. My family was discouraged too. They had worked right alongside me these months, demolishing, cleaning, working hard to see our dreams come true. And right about the time we should have been celebrating our success, was the time we were wondering if it would ever end.

# PART THREE: THE MEETINGS

# CHAPTER EIGHT

About two months into the remodel, we were on our family vacation. We take one every year to the Central Oregon area to visit family. While we were on vacation, I felt like it was a good time to sit down with my two kids, who were in their early teens at that time, and explain to them what had taken place. I felt that they were old enough to be a part of the decision and the action that would follow. My kids, Adam and Megan, were very familiar with the house and what had been going on with the remodel. They had helped on some of the easier jobs at the house and of course, I had come home with tales of all the complications and issues that we had experienced. They had put a lot of time in there and I was so proud of their work. It really had become a family project and so they were personally involved just as much as I was. I explained to them what I found, where I had found it and what the attorneys had to say. I had planned to give them the opportunity to give their opinions on what should happen with the money, but before I could share my perspective, Megan had already made up her mind.

"The attorneys said that since we could identify who put it there, that it belongs to them, right?"

"Yes, Megan, that's what they said. They also said that no one could force us to give the money to Mr. Bell's heirs."

"Well there is no question, Dad, it's not our money. We have to give it to Mr. Bell's daughters."

I sat in silence after she had spoken. I knew at that moment that this was all going to be worth it. I looked at Adam.

"Right." He said. "It's just not ours. It's as simple as that, Dad."

I smiled and nodded at my kids, not trusting myself to speak at that moment. I have never been prouder of them than at that moment.

\#

The year in question was a family reunion year, so we had a lot of family there where we were taking our vacation. We shared the story with our family. We told them what our project was, what we had found and what the details were. We also shared the fact that we had decided to give the money to Mr. Bell's daughters as they were his legal heirs. We talked about how we had met and talked to the Bell Sisters and what they were like. It was an incredible opportunity to witness to friends and family about the experience of it and what it meant for us as well as sharing how complicated and tempting it was to keep the money. Discussing with those close to us the emotions that were involved was liberating. But the bottom line was that it is all about doing the right thing. Regardless of the fact that we were way upside down at this point in this house and most likely going to lose money, it wasn't about us, it was about them; his daughters.

\#

When we got home from our family vacation, I started doing a lot of market research on the currency I had found to determine what the value of it was. I proceeded to try to find out as much as I possibly could about the old currency, what the fair market value was. We had heard what the legal answers were, and we knew what the moral and spiritual answers were, so now it was just a matter of finding the right time. I really, really wanted to wait until the house was done, because I wanted to have the two daughters over to the house to explain everything to them. However, with the setbacks we had experienced in getting the house finished, the time when it would be officially 'completed' kept being further and further into the future. Not wanting to wait any longer, I decided to make contact with the Bell Sisters. We had returned from our trip and I just decided that there was no use in putting it off any longer. Now was as good a time as any to give the sisters Harold's gift to them. It wasn't doing us any good to hold on to the treasures any longer and it would do them all the good in the world to have it.

I called the older sister, Karen, and told her I would like for her and her sister to come over to the house so we could meet with them. She gave me all kinds of excuses as to why it wasn't going to be convenient and they would have to come at separate times and that her sister is wheelchair bound and it would just be impossible for them to come any time soon.

"Karen, we would really like to have you and Rose over to the house so you can get a tour and see all the changes we've made. I'd love to hear your thoughts on the remodel efforts."

"Well, Larry, that's very sweet of you and of course, we would love to but it's so difficult with Rosey being in the wheelchair now. It's hard to get her to go anywhere and then it's hard to get her in and out of the car. It's rough on all of us to go out somewhere."

"It's really important that you come and see the house. I need to talk to you about something."

"I just don't know. I guess we might be able to come out next week or so. Maybe the week after, depending on how the weather looks. You know, I don't like to drive in bad weather and the weather man said there could be rain in the next few weeks. It's just so stressful, Larry, you know."

I sighed and tried again. "It's really important to you also, that you come see the house, Karen."

She was silent and I thought she had hung up on me. Finally she answered.

"You found it, didn't you?" She almost whispered.

"What do you mean?" I asked innocently.

"You found the money." She all but breathed into the receiver.

"We did find something that I believe belonged to your Father and I would like to return it to you and your sister."

"You found the money! Oh my goodness. Rosey and I looked for years for that money."

She proceeded to explain to me that they knew their dad always dealt in cash and had cash in his pockets. She said he always had little storage spots around the house for cash and goodies. If he heard their mom needed money for something, he would disappear for several minutes and then come back with money for their Mother, his wife. On his deathbed, he was talking with Karen in his last moments and he said, "You've got to go home and get the money." After she left the hospital that night, he passed away quietly. The sisters never did find out from Harold where the money was that they were supposed to retrieve. So the sisters knew there was money to be found but they didn't know how much or where it was. They kept the house for two years after he passed away in the hopes of finding the money he had spoken of. They thought the money was in his belongings. Harold had been a collector of stuff, and he had a lot of stuff all over the house and garage. They thought the money was hidden in some of his collected items and they spent years going through it all but they never found any of it. As a result, the money had haunted them since his passing. The sisters finally decided they just needed to sell the house and let it go because they were never going to find the money and hanging on to the house was costing them money. So they had some minor repairs done on the house and had it cleaned up and put on the market. They sold the house to the person that I bought it from.

While Karen and I talked about the treasure and what was in the papers, she asked me if I had found a ring.

"Did you find the ring?" Her voice was quiet and still but I could tell this ring was important to her.

"No, I don't think there was a ring. What did it look like?" Obviously I knew what a ring was, but something told me to ask.

"It was a simple ring with a diamond in it. Dad stored it in a wooden box."

"Hmm." I said, thinking. "I don't remember a wooden box."

"Well, you would remember this one. It had carvings on it I guess."

"Was it an important ring?" I asked her.

"It's just that Rosey has been dreaming about it. When Rose was small, she was with Dad when he bought the ring for our Mother. Rose asked him if she could have it someday and he promised her that she would have it later in her life. He never mentioned it to either of us before he died, but Rose has been dreaming about the ring and Dad over and over ever since he died."

"Really?" I asked, riveted by the story of the ring and box.

"Yes. Apparently, in the dream, he is telling her to look in the wooden box with the carvings."

Immediately, the block of wood with carvings on it sprung to mind. It must actually be a box. I wanted to surprise the girls with the ring, so I kept it to myself for the moment that I did indeed have the box. I wanted to be sure the ring was in it before I got their hopes up.

We talked some more about her dad and I shared a little bit with her about what we had found and what I had researched about all the currency and so forth. I told her what was involved and how much was involved, and she was in awe about the whole thing. She said she would talk to her sister and then get back to me about a date, but they would prefer to do it at her house because of the handicap accessibility issue with the remodeled house. We agreed to that and I waited to hear back from her.

# CHAPTER NINE

Right after my conversation with Karen, I hung up the phone and ran out to my tool shed where the bags of empty containers were. I tore through the bags and containers, looking for the wooden block. At the first pass, I didn't find it. I panicked, trying to remember if maybe I had thrown it out after all. It was getting dark in the shed, so I turned on the light and sat on the stool. I grabbed the bags one by one and started methodically searching each and every trash bag for a can that rattled until I found the carving. I pulled it out and looked at it, but it was too dark in the shed. I brought the wooden block inside the house and into the kitchen where the lights were the brightest. I turned the block over and over in my hands, gently pulling at it in opposite directions as I turned it. Although the hard wood held carvings and symbols that scarred its surface, the box somehow felt soft. The wood looked old and aged, like many hands had worked this box, perhaps trying to discover its secret just as I was doing now. At just the right angle, the sides pulled apart gently and I could see where the two pieces of wood slid together to create a cube. I carefully pulled the box open wider and tilted the interior towards the light. There was nothing inside. As I tried to close the box again, it felt like it was sticking and wouldn't close. I knocked the box against the edge of the kitchen counter to loosen the tracks that slid the box together and apart. Something bounced out onto the floor, making a tinging sound. I stood looking down at the biggest diamond ring I have ever seen. It shone and winked at me from the light on the ceiling. I stood looking down at it for a few moments, almost afraid to pick it up. Finally, I bent down and grabbed it gingerly between thumb and forefinger. Holding it up to the light, I could tell it was a real stone and that it was big.

I searched around for something safe to put it in. Finding only a plastic bag with a zipper, I put the ring inside and put it into my pocket. That afternoon I had some errands to do, so I took the ring with me to the mall and I went into one of the local jewelers. I explained that I had found the ring and was just curious about what the ring was worth. The woman behind the counter looked at it pursed her lips together. She glanced at me but said nothing. She reached into a small drawer by the register and got out one of those little eye monocles. Putting the monocle in place, she peered at the ring, turning it this way and that way under the lamp on the counter. Her eye looked huge through the glass of the eye piece and I stopped myself from chuckling as I waited. She glanced at me, placed the ring on a velvet pillow in front of me and said she'd be right back. She went into the back of the store and emerged with another store employee. The man looked at it, used a monocle, just like the woman had and then called someone else over to look at the ring. I was getting nervous about the whole thing. What if they thought I had stolen it? What if it was junk and they thought I was pulling a prank to waste their time? Pretty soon every employee in the store was looking at it and some customers were getting curious too. The woman could tell that all the attention was making me uncomfortable.

"Well, Mr. Campbell," the woman said, placing the ring in a velvet bag and handing it back to me. "If I had to guess, I'd say that ring is worth about $30,000. Minimum."

I was speechless. I knew it was a large diamond, but I had no idea it would be worth that much.

"Are you sure?" I stammered, in awe of her words.

She quirked an eyebrow at me, "Pretty sure." She glanced at the other store employees who had also looked at the ring and they all nodded their agreement.

"Wow." Was all I could think to say. I thanked them for their time and exited the store, with the ring safely tucked into my pocket.

The very next day, I added the ring to the currency being stored in the safe deposit box at the bank. I was so glad I hadn't thrown the block of wood out. It just goes to show you that if something doesn't belong to you, you may not know its true value. And also, don't throw anything away until you're sure of its value.

A few days later, I heard back from Karen and we set up a time to meet her and Rose about a week later at Karen's house. I took my wife and my kids with me and we took the more rare currency that I had separated out and put into the binder. We got the ring from the safe deposit box and took that with us as well as some of the coins. We arrived at Karen's house and got out of the car. Her home was sedate and non-eventful in an average subdivision. Purple and yellow pansies marched up the walk on either side of the path. It was hard to imagine anyone owning this home growing up in the one I had spent the last several months remodeling. It was like comparing Plain Jane to the Queen of England.

Karen answered the door and invited us all in to her warm home. We were shown into the living room where Rose was already. She was seated on the love seat, her wheelchair close by. The room was clean and well cared for. The furniture was nice, but obviously older. The curtains were open, letting in our daily dose of sunshine. Once we were all seated comfortably and refreshments had been taken care of, I explained the story as it happened. I explained the whole process of being drawn to the basement room, of starting to remove the wall treatment in just the right spot, finding the money and all I had gone through to bring it to them in the end. I told them what my attorneys had said and how I determined the treasure trove had belonged to their father. The sisters were overwhelmed. They sat together on the love seat across from me and my family who had all sat on the couch. The sisters were sitting close to one another and holding hands while their free hands clutched tissues. There was a lot of crying, a lot of tears shed, a lot of talk about their dad and the fact that finally they could close the chapter on the money and this mysterious part of their lives. There was also a huge portion of disbelief that it was real and we were real and we were really doing this. I mean, who would do this when you could just keep it for yourself and not tell anyone?

I was feeling the burden of the money start to be released from my soul. This money was theirs and they deserved it and soon this part of the adventure would be all over. I had consulted with my attorney when I decided to give the money back and he had advised me to have them sign a release. So, all I asked of the sisters was that before we turned over the money I wanted a legal document signed by everyone involved that held me totally void of any responsibility for this inheritance from their father. The document would include everything that was found and state that it belonged to them and that I was giving it to them of my own free will. They agreed to sign the forms and we made arrangements for that. Then once that was taken care of through our attorneys, we scheduled a time to meet them at our bank and I took the two of them into the safe deposit box room. I showed them the contents and turned over the keys. What a huge burden that was to be lifted off my shoulders, my family's shoulders, that responsibility as well as the temptation and the desire for it to be something different than what it was, was suddenly gone. It was a solemn moment when I passed the treasure over to the girls and turned my back on all that fortune.

A few weeks after I had turned over the findings to their rightful owners, Karen called me up out of the blue.

"Larry?" She asked over the phone lines.

"Yes, Karen. How are you?"

"Oh we are fine, Larry, just fine thank you. Rose and I are so grateful to you for what you did for us. We just can't believe someone could be that good and kind."

"Oh." I didn't quite know what to say. "Don't worry about it, Karen. I'm glad to do it."

The line was silent for a few seconds.

"Karen?" I said, "Are you still there?"

"Yes," I could hear her sniff, she was crying, "I'm here. I'm sorry. We just are so grateful to you. I can't tell you what a huge difference this money has made in our lives. It's a blessing, Larry, truly a blessing. You're a blessing."

"Thanks, Karen, really. I'm glad. It's good to know I made the right decision."

"Oh, you did! You absolutely made the right decision. Rose and I just cannot believe our luck. We had thought the mystery of our Father's money would be forever unsolved. It just means so much to us that we have solved the riddle of the money and the ring. We would like to give you a reward."

I could hear the excitement in her voice and knew this was something she was happy about.

"A reward?" I asked, "You don't have to do that, Karen. I don't expect it."

"I know you don't expect it. That's why we want to give it to you."

"Well, that's very kind of you and Rose, Karen. Thank you very much."

"I'll send you a check, Larry. What's your mailing address?"

I gave her my mailing address and there was a reward involved. I didn't lose all the money after all. The money I received from the sisters was just enough to cover the repairs to the basement from the flooding. So we recovered the costs for the expenses of materials for the flooded basement, which was very helpful at the time because that was all out-of-pocket expense. I did most of the work myself on the repairs so the reward money the sisters gave me covered all the expense that related to the basement damage.

Although I received a small amount of help with the expenses of repairing the house, there was, however, the immediate need to sell the house and make some cash. Every month that went by that I remained the owner of that house was a month where I spent 4,500 dollars on the loan payment. I needed to get this house sold and fast. The housing market was still in the gutter and I knew a house as expensive as this one was not really going to be on the top of everyone's list. It was beautiful when it was finished, and I knew people would love it. But would they be able to afford something of this size and price range? In this economy? With the disclosures we had on this house? It wasn't looking good, but I was trying to remain optimistic.

Regardless of doing the right thing, you still question yourself, you still question whether it was all worth it. Especially in the situation I found myself in. I was hemorrhaging money with no end in sight. I had been drawn to this house, drawn to the basement and driven to get inside that wall. I had given the girls the money that their Father had intended for them and I had finished remodeling the house. Why was this happening to us? At times, I doubted that I did the right thing by returning the money to Karen and Rose. But then I remembered her voice telling me how it had changed their lives and how grateful they both were. I knew I had done the right thing and that warmed my heart, but in the meanwhile, my bank account was definitely going cold.

# CHAPTER TEN

In the next few months, as we continued to try and sell the house, I became more and more frustrated. I was talking to a co-worker of mine at my regular day job, Candice, about the situation. She knew a little about real estate and knew I was flipping a house and that I had hit some road bumps with the project.

"So no one's interested?" She asked when I told her the dilemma.

"No, it's not that. I don't know what it is." I said in frustration. "People come through, they say they love the house and then nothing. Just nothing. No offer, no conversation, no nothing."

"Really? That's weird. Not one offer?"

"No, not one. And yes, it is weird."

She was quiet for a moment while she thought about what might be happening and then she looked at me with a grin on her face.

"You know what you need, Larry?"

"A buyer for my house?"

She chuckled.

"Yes, but in order to get a buyer for your house, you need something else."

"What's that?" I asked, ready to try anything.

"You need a house blessing."

I'm pretty sure she heard the disbelief in my thoughts as I stared at her.

"A what?" I said.

"A house blessing." She said. "It's when you have somebody come through your house and bless it because you must have spirits there that are running everybody off."

I waited for a few moments to see if she was joking.

Reading my mind, she said, "I'm not joking, Larry. You need a house blessing."

I was desperate enough at that point in time that I was willing to try almost anything.

"Okay," I told her, "let's schedule it."

As a gift, Candice wanted to pay for the house blessing. So we decided to go ahead with it. Candice said she knew of a medium who did house blessings and cleansing services. Candice called up the medium, Theresa, and arranged to make payment on my behalf. So, Candice paid Theresa to come to the house and said she would have me call her to give her the details and set the appointment.

When I got home from work that evening, I told my wife about what Candice had said. She was silent for a moment and then she looked as if she would say something, but she didn't. She was at a loss for words.

Finally, Sarah laughed and said, "A Medium, Larry?"

"I know, I know. But we've tried everything else and nothing is working."

Sarah chuckled again, "Do you think there are ghosts in the house, Larry? And they're keeping people from buying the house?"

"I don't know. But I know I'm going to do everything I can to sell this house. If a house blessing will make people more confident in the thing, then so be it. Besides, I didn't even have to pay for it, so what can it hurt?"

"You didn't have to pay for it?" She asked.

"No, Candice and I were talking about the house issues and she offered to pay for it as a house completion gift for us."

"Oh. Well I guess we can't argue with that, huh?"

"That's what I thought."

We both laughed a little over the thought of having a Medium in to do a house blessing. But we both knew if we didn't get rid of this house soon, we were going to have a huge problem, so we were also willing to try anything.

I called Theresa the next day, when I was off work and had some free time.

"Hello, this is Theresa." She sounded pleasant when she answered her phone.

"Hi, Theresa, this is Larry Campbell. My friend Candice Humphreys called you yesterday about a house blessing?"

"Yes, of course. How are you Mr. Campbell?"

"Please, call me Larry. And I'm good. How are you today?"

"I'm great, Larry. Thanks for asking." There was a pause and I heard some paper shuffling then she asked, "When do you want the blessing to be done?"

"As soon as possible would be great."

"This weekend is okay for you, then?"

"Yes, that would be great."

"Excellent, I'll put you down on Saturday, then. What time would you like me to meet you at the house?"

"How about 1 o'clock?"

"That's perfect. And what is the address please?"

I gave her the address and she noted it down along with my cell phone number.

"Great. So I will see you on Saturday at 1 o'clock at the house. Okay, Larry?"

"Yes, I look forward to it."

"See you then. Bye bye." She ended the call.

It didn't really occur to me until later that she didn't ask any questions about the house or the situation. I thought that was odd. I mean, wouldn't she want to know what she was getting herself into? I guess she was the professional and knew what she was doing. So I put the appointment on my calendar and waited with trepidation until Saturday.

When my wife got home that evening, I told her about the appointment and what time I was meeting Theresa at the house.

"Do you want to go?" I asked her.

"No, not unless you need me there for moral support."

"Ha, Ha." I glared at her. "I'll be fine. Thank you very much."

Sarah laughed as she began preparing dinner.

"Do you know anything about house blessings?" She asked me with her head inside the fridge.

"No," I sat on the barstool at the kitchen counter, "Not really. Do you?"

"No. Definitely not." She brought some food to the counter and began gathering utensils and spices for what she was about to cook.

"Maybe I should do a little research so I know what to expect, you know?"

"Yeah, that's a good idea. At least then you won't be surprised if she goes into a trance or starts to have convulsions or something." Sarah laughed at the horrified look that must have been on my face.

"That doesn't happen, does it?" I asked, incredulously.

"I don't know, Larry. I've never been to a house blessing. I'm just teasing you."

I shot her another look as I left the kitchen to do some research before dinner was ready.

What I found out was that a house blessing was a religious ceremony where the person performing the ritual comes and says prayers throughout the house to cleanse it of evil spirits or energies. Priests and other holy people had performed such ceremonies for hundreds of years. In some instances, apparently, the person performing the ritual might put oils or other items in the rooms of the house as they worked. The elements of the oil or fragrance were said to be holy and aided in the removal of spirits.

As I read more information, I discovered that some people who do house blessings for others do pretend to be inhabited by spirits or may actually be inhabited by spirits. I had to admit that this information freaked me out a little bit and I called Candice to talk with her about Theresa.

"Hey, Candice, it's Larry."

"Hi, Larry. What's up?"

"Hey, I was just doing some research on house blessings and I…"

"Uh oh. You weren't reading stuff on the Internet were you?" She laughed.

"Yes, I was actually. Why?"

"Well, you can't believe everything you read."

"True. Still, have you had Theresa do a house blessing for you personally?" I told Candice about what I had read on the Internet about some Mediums being possessed by the spirits they were trying to evacuate.

"Yeah, sure. Every time I move to a new place or have a friend who has moved to a new place, I have Theresa do a house blessing. I've used her for years and she has never been possessed or had seizures or anything."

I was silent for a moment, thinking about what she had said.

"Larry?"

"Yeah, I'm here."

"I promise she's not going to do anything over the top weird. She comes in, puts some flowers and oil around, maybe some fragrance, depending on what she feels is necessary. Then she goes through the house saying prayers and blessings. That's it."

"Really?"

"Yes, really. You can go with her through the house or you can wait somewhere, whatever you're comfortable with."

"Okay. That's good. Do you go with her or do you wait?"

"I go with her. It's interesting to hear her say what she finds and what she's feeling and stuff."

"What does she find or feel?"

"Well, she usually finds spirits in the house and she can feel if they're angry or sad and stuff like that."

"Oh." I said, not sure how I felt about that.

"It's not as bad as you think it is, Larry. She's very practical and doesn't make it all dramatic or weird."

"Okay," I said. "My appointment is on Saturday at 1 o'clock."

"Oh good, she was able to see you soon, that's great. Well, call me when it's done and let me know how it went."

"Ok, I will. And, thanks, Candice."

"You're welcome, Larry. I hope it helps. And tell Sarah I said hello!"

"Will do. Bye."

I hung up feeling both a little better and a little more nervous about the impending appointment with Theresa VanCoolidge. I hoped all went well and there was no weirdness. I wasn't really the kind of guy who liked drama and weirdness. This was all a little outside of my comfort zone here and I was feeling apprehensive about the whole thing. Still, I had known Candice for a few years and she was pretty down to Earth. If Candice said Theresa was okay, then I would go into it with an open mind.

I walked back into the kitchen and told Sarah about my research and my conversation with Candice. Sarah felt the same way I did and now definitely did not want to be in the house when the house blessing happened. We talked a little as we finished getting dinner ready together and I felt much better by the time it was time to eat.

That evening, as I went to bed, I prayed that the house blessing would help the karma in the house and that we would sell it soon. I spent some time being grateful for all that I had and all that my family had. I silently offered up my praise and love and went to bed hopeful that Saturday would bring some answers and some relief.

# PART FOUR: THE GHOST

# CHAPTER ELEVEN

The day of the appointment came and I was pretty nervous. A little blue compact vehicle pulled up to the curb, not the Volkswagen bus I had imagined. The car door opened and she stepped out. She was not what I had expected at all. I had always pictured Mediums as weirdos with hippy clothing talking about love and peace and spirits from the other side making contact with flowers in their un-brushed hair. This Medium apparently didn't get the weirdo memo on how to dress and make people feel uncomfortable. Theresa was wearing a light gray sweater and black slacks. She had shoulder length brown hair and brown eyes. She looked normal. She looked just like a normal person that would be anywhere. She was not familiar to me, we had never met before and I knew she had never been to the house before. She didn't have any previous knowledge of the house and the only things she even knew about the house was what she could see with her own eyes. When we had talked on the phone, I had told her that I had a house that I had remodeled and that I had recently put that house up for sale. That's all she knew. She smiled as we shook hands and I motioned her toward the front door of the house. She had a black case on wheels that she pulled behind her as she walked into the house. I followed her in and she stood in the front hallway quietly for a moment before moving into the living room area.

She opened her case and I could see various items in there. She had some small glass plates, packages of what looked like potpourri, some candles, and various other bottles, bags and containers of things. She removed a paper wrapped bag from the case and as she unwrapped the paper, I could see there were fresh flowers in the bag. Theresa started setting up her items. She put a dish in each room of the house with a candle, some incense and some fresh cut flowers on each plate. Once that was all set up, she proceeded to walk through the house clearing out the spirits. She moved slowly, waving a burnt bundle of sage in the air. She said it would clear energies from the house that shouldn't be there. The smell of the smoldering sage was pleasant. I stayed in the kitchen while she went through the house.

When she came back to the kitchen after her first time through, she stopped on the other side of the room from me and stood there with a curious look on her face for a moment. Then she slowly smiled and started laughing.

"What's going on?" I asked.

"Well, there is a very upset elderly man standing next to you and he is not very happy."

I looked to my right, in the direction she had pointed. I didn't see anything.

"I don't see anything." I said.

"He's there, next to you. He is not being belligerent and he is not cussing or anything like that, but he is very angry. He is very upset. He wants to know why you did all these things to his house."

"I," I started to explain myself, but I didn't know what to say. "I remodeled it." It wasn't an explanation, but I didn't know what to say. I had made the house better.

Theresa laughed. "He doesn't think that's a good answer."

"It was outdated. I bought the house as an investment, made some improvements and now I'm trying to sell it for a profit."

She was quiet, looking at the empty space next to me as if she was listening.

"He says he understands, but he's still not happy about all the changes you've made."

She then described to me how tall the man was and what he looked like. I knew that she was talking about Harold even before she explained that this was his house and that he had built the house and that he didn't appreciate anything that I had done to it. He was upset. He didn't like all the people coming through the house either. Neither the workers or the people looking at the house to hopefully buy it. He was just beside himself, a very unhappy camper.

Theresa and I then went from room to room, starting with the main floor. As we entered each room, Theresa would explain what the room had been used for, the history of the room and what Harold loved about each one. We went into one of the bedrooms and she told me about it in words that came from the ghost.

"This room belonged to two girls, his daughters. There was a bed here." She spread her hands out, showing me where one bed would have sat. "And one here." She moved to the other side of the room and spread her hands in the air by the wall again. She looked past my shoulder toward the doorway and nodded her head.

"And this," She moved toward the end of the room where the window was. "Was where he had put in a window seat for the girls to sit and read. They loved to read." Theresa smiled wistfully as if she were speaking of her own children. "He loved them very much."

We went into the other bedroom.

"This was the master bedroom. This was his room. He and his wife lived in here, slept in here." She stood in silence for a moment, her head bowed. She was silent for several minutes and I began to get nervous.

"Are you alright?" I asked, afraid she was going to go into a trance or something.

"Yes." She raised her head and smiled. "He is so sad. He loved his wife very much. He can't bear to be in this room without her."

We went through the living room where I had removed all the paneling. She stopped in the middle of the room, a small smile playing at the corners of her mouth.

"You removed wood from the walls in here." She said matter of fact like.

"Yes. I did." I said.

"He is not very happy about the wood that was taken down and the paneling that was removed." She chuckled and walked from the room.

I was shocked and impressed, to put it lightly. Theresa had never seen the house before, she had no way of knowing that the room we were in had previously had paneling in it and that I had removed all of that wood during my remodeling process.

In the kitchen, Theresa said Harold was so angry at me that he refused to even speak to her. Her brows were furrowed with concern and she darted her eyes at me. Her look was almost accusatory.

"What did you do in here?"

"Uh... I..." I stammered, trying to remember what all we had done in the kitchen. "Well, we removed some tile..."

Before I could finish listing out all the work we had done in the kitchen, Theresa's eyes shot to a spot near the doorway. She nodded her head up and down. She was silent for a moment, and so was I, sensing I was no longer what she was listening to and that her attention was focused somewhere else. After a few minutes, she turned her gaze to me.

"The tile." She said. "The tile was imported marble from Italy. He is furious with you for taking it out and trashing it like it was nothing. That was his most prized part of the house. That Italian marble."

"It was damaged... I had to replace it..." I turned my gaze toward the doorway where I had seen Theresa looking. "I'm sorry." I said.

I fell silent, feeling terrible for making Harold so upset.

"It's a great house, Harold. You did a wonderful job. I was just trying to make it even better. It's beautiful." I said quietly in the direction I hoped he was in.

The room was silent again and finally Theresa spoke, "He forgives you." She smiled a serene smile and we continued to another room.

The rest of the house went in pretty much the same pattern. We would enter a room and she would tell me about the room, how it been when Harold had built it and what I had changed since purchasing the house. She would tell me what Harold was saying and I swear there was not a room that he wasn't angry with me about. Finally, we went downstairs into the basement.

"This is his space." She walked into the center of the main basement area. Lifting her hands slightly from her sides, she tilted her head up and closed her eyes. She looked like a human sundial or something, like she was soaking up the suns rays. "This is where he lived and it is also where he is currently staying."

She stood silently in the middle of the room for a few more minutes. Then she smiled and opened her eyes.

"This is where he feels safe and loved. After his wife died, he was here all the time. His daughters were gone and he was alone after that. He couldn't bare being in that big empty house all by himself, so he just stayed down here. Content to be alone where the others' memories didn't linger."

I felt sorry for Harold then. I imagined him, an old man. His children had grown and gone off to live their own lives. His wife passed away, the love of his life. And here he was, in this huge house all by himself. Just him and his treasure. He must have stayed down here to guard the money, to make sure it was safe and that no one could get to it. It was for his daughters. It was their inheritance when he died and he wanted it to be intact and safe for them.

Theresa was watching me, watching the thoughts flit across my face. When she saw me look up at her, she smiled.

"Do you feel it?" She asked solemnly.

"Feel what?"

"His sorrow. His pain. His loneliness."

"I don't know if I feel it necessarily, but I can sympathize. I feel bad for him."

She smiled at me again and turned to walk into the rest of the basement, waving her still smoldering bundle of sage and whispering prayers and blessings. I followed behind her, anxious to see and hear what she would discover in the other basement rooms.

In one room, Harold was unhappy about the brick we had covered up. He had loved the way the brick looked. He thought it was very classic and elegant. I told him, through her (I still didn't really want to talk to the air), that brick was outdated. It was discolored and we had to cover it because it wasn't practical to redo the brick. In another room, he was mad that we had taken out the shower. He had put that in himself and was rather proud of it. I explained to him that it was out of place because there wasn't a bathroom down here, just a solitary shower. It was sort of weird. He didn't like that, but I think he was beginning to respect my opinion about the way the house had been remodeled.

After circling back to the main basement area, Theresa and I were standing next to one another in the center of the big main room. This was the room she had identified as Harold's space, the place he had spent most of his time after his wife had passed away. His sanctuary, if you will. We stood, looking around silently and just sort of soaking in all we had seen and heard during the cleansing of the house. I was standing with my face pointed toward the open doorway to the Treasure Room. Theresa had said nothing while we had been in that room and I was surprised that Harold had not mentioned the money that had been hidden there. Did he know we had found the money and returned it to Karen and Rose? Or did he think the money was still there? I was about to ask Theresa about the room to see if Harold would tell her anything without me having to when I had a weird feeling come over my body.

I felt like I was about to be attacked. I spun around, looking behind me for the force of energy I had felt there a moment ago. I looked at Theresa. She was smiling an odd smile and the hair on the back of my neck stood on end.

# CHAPTER TWELVE

It was the weirdest feeling I had ever experienced in my life. I had heard the phrase hundreds of times, but had never experienced it for myself. It's one of those feelings that you don't truly understand when somebody else mentions it but you know exactly what they were talking about the second it happens to you. I was looking at Theresa, wondering why she was smiling and barely concealing her laughter when the feeling came again.

The entire back side of my body went cold and it felt like someone was brushing my neck with a feather. I swatted at the back of my neck and whirled around. I didn't see anything. I glanced up to see if air was coming from the vents or an open window. I was in the middle of the room. There were no vents or fans near me and no open windows to speak of. Slowly, I turned to look at Theresa again.

She looked back at me and she started laughing. My arms broke out in goose bumps.

"What's going on?" I asked her and was surprised to hear a slight quaver in my voice. I was startled.

"Harold is here, Larry. He is standing behind you."

"He is? My back just felt cold a second ago." I rubbed my lower back, trying to make the chill go away.

"People typically do feel coldness when a spirit or 'ghost' is near them. It's alright, that's normal." She smiled.

I felt the movement against my neck again and the hair on the back of my neck just stood on end. I swatted my neck again and glanced around.

"He is blowing on the back of your neck." Theresa was chuckling.

"What?!" I jerked out of the way, moving to stand beside Theresa again, my hand firmly planted on the back of my neck.

"Why is he doing that?" I asked her.

"I'm not sure. Maybe he is just trying to get your attention. And you can't see him or hear him so he is trying to use another method."

"Can you ask him to stop that? It's really creeping me out." I said to her.

"He can hear you, Larry. He will stop. But he wants you to listen to what he has to say."

"Okay. I'm listening."

Theresa listened to Harold for a few moments. She nodded her head and murmured her understanding. Finally, she looked at me.

"All he really wants more than anything is for his house to be back the way it was. Then he would be happy and he would quit bothering people." Theresa was silent for a few moments. She was listening, or so I guessed, to Harold.

"What does he mean 'bothering people'?" I asked.

"Well, he really liked you in the beginning. He chose you to be the owner of this house when you came through to look at it because he knew he could influence you. He knew you were a good man and that he could get you to follow his guidance." I grimaced at that comment but continued listening. "He put ideas in your mind as far as the things he did want changed in the house."

Instantly I was thinking of the wall in the treasury room, the wall that I never would have taken down had I been left to my own devices. But as soon as I had that house it became an obsession for me. I never understood why I had been so obsessed with making that closet in the Treasure Room, even though after the money had been found, I never did make the closet in there. Now it all made sense, that Harold had obviously put that series of thoughts into my mind to have me discover his treasure trove. My attention returned to Theresa when she began speaking again.

"He is also mentioning that he does not like all the people coming through the house. He just wants it all to stop. He wants you to go away. He tried to make you go away on your own, but you wouldn't go."

"He tried to make me go away?" I questioned that last comment.

"Yes." She was silent for a moment, listening and nodding her head. "Apparently, he caused the basement to flood. He thought for sure that you would not come back after that. He was pretty sure that would be the last straw and you would put an end to all of it."

This made a lot of sense to me. While talking to Karen's husband, I had found out that there was a storm drain that would plug up from time to time and would need to be cleaned out periodically at the house. Coincidentally, it was the very same drain that had overflowed and caused the flooding in the basement. It was an ongoing issue, something that Harold was knowledgeable of and obviously had some influence in when we had those torrential downpours. The flooding and subsequent repair work did shut down the open houses for about six weeks, so he did accomplish something with his antics, I guess.

Theresa continued to talk to Harold, trying to see if she could reason with him. She suggested he cross over to the other side and leave his presence here in our world, but he wouldn't have anything to do with it.

"He absolutely does not want to leave this house." She said.

We talked back and forth for a while with her telling me what he had said and me telling her what to tell him even though he could hear me just fine. But all the talk in the world wasn't going to do any good. Nothing was going to make him leave that house.

Theresa sighed, "I was hoping not to have to do this." She said.

"Do what?" I asked curiously.

"I could try to summon his wife and see if she could get him to leave and go with her to the other side."

I stared at her in silence for a moment. This was all getting pretty weird for me. Over the course of a few hours, I had started to believe in this house blessing thing. Theresa had mentioned things and known things about the house that she could not have known if Harold had not truly been the one telling her the information. My opinion had been swayed in that regard. But summoning a spirit? I did not think I was quite ready for that one.

"You can do that?" I said.

"Well, I can try." She said. "Honestly, it doesn't always work, but I have done it before and sometimes it is very effective if the spirit that is here and the spirit that has passed over had a strong bond. Harold is torn. He does not want us to call Esther because he doesn't want to leave this house. But he also loves her very much and would like to see her and speak with her again."

"Well," I heard myself saying, "go ahead and try it I guess."

Theresa went upstairs to her case to get some supplies and returned a few moments later. She lit some white candles and placed them in a big circle on the floor with her and I inside it. She was reciting prayers quietly as she lit and placed the candles. I was nervous, very nervous. I had never been exposed to anything like this before and I could barely believe it was happening now. I was quiet and watched her as she moved around and prayed. Finally she looked at me and smiled and came to stand beside me.

"The prayers and white candles are here to protect us. We will ask Esther to join us and see if she will come. Are you ready?"

"Yes."

She took my hand and bowed her head. I bowed mine as well, and following her lead, I closed my eyes.

"Esther Bell." Theresa began in a strong but gentle voice. "Please join us here. Esther Bell, we are in need of your help and guidance for your husband Harold Bell. Please come and speak with us. We wish you no harm."

We waited for a moment and Theresa repeated her call to Esther. I kept my head down, not trusting myself to look up. I think I was secretly hoping it didn't work, but then I realized it may be the only way to get Harold out of there so we could sell the house successfully. As Theresa called to Esther over and over, I felt the gentle touch on my neck again. This time I did not jump and it did not scare me. This time I think I felt a little of his sorrow, his longing for his dead wife and the need to be at peace.

Almost as soon as I had this realization about Harold, I felt a cold chill in front of me. Theresa squeezed my hand softly.

"She is here." She whispered.

I opened my eyes and looked around. I didn't see anything new, but I could feel the presence. I could feel an energy in the room. It's like when you have been waiting for someone and you hear their footsteps in the hallway. I didn't hear anything, but I had the feeling that my waiting was almost at an end.

"Do you see her?" Theresa asked me quietly.

I shook my head no. "But I think I feel something."

"She has a very strong presence."

"Thank you, Esther, for coming to speak with us." Theresa began. "Your husband, Harold, is in need of your help. He has trapped himself in this Earthly prison and needs your gentle guidance to lead him forward into his afterlife."

She was silent, listening and looking near a spot in the center of the circle of candles. I assumed that's where Esther was.

Theresa leaned toward me and whispered, "They are talking to each other." She informed me.

We waited. I couldn't see what was going on, and I couldn't hear the ghosts speaking to one another. I patiently waited and finally Theresa told me what was going on.

"Esther is trying to convince Harold to go with her, to pass over. He is strongly attached to this house, but he loves her and wants to be with her. Esther wants my help now as well."

Theresa took a step closer to the center of the circle.

"Harold." She said gently. "The afterlife is nothing to be afraid of. Once you pass over, you will have everything the way you want. You will have your house back the way it was and you will have Esther by your side. Your house and your wife will stay the way you want them to forever more, Harold. You can change things if you want or leave them they way they were when you passed away."

Theresa listened for a moment. "Esther is agreeing with what I've said. She is telling him it's true. That he can have things however he wants them if he crosses over."

We waited for a few moments more as husband and wife discussed their options.

"He has agreed to go with her. Harold has agreed to go with Esther." Theresa said with a smile on her face.

At that moment, I wished that I could see them. I wished that I could hear the words they spoke to one another. Spirits no longer of our physical world speaking to one another, having a conversation about crossing over. I pictured them standing together, facing one another, hands clasped. Suddenly, I wished I had the ability to witness this incredible event happening. But regardless of my inability to see or hear it, it sounded like it had worked. Harold's love for Esther had won out and he was willing to leave the house and cross over to begin his afterlife with her in the house he wanted.

"Wait," Theresa said. "He has a stipulation."

I was afraid of what it may be. What would this old man ask for? This man who had kept me from realizing my dreams and was costing me money I couldn't afford to lose. This man who should be gone and wasn't from our world. What could he possibly want? And was I prepared to give it?

# CHAPTER THIRTEEN

The suspense was killing me as Theresa listened to Harold. I waited as patiently as possible, but it was really hard. My mind was racing, trying to imagine all the things a ghost would ask of a living being. I didn't have to wait long thankfully.

"He wants to make sure that whoever does buy his house understands how important the house was to him and how much hard work he put into it. He wants you to promise him that you will tell the new owners how much he loved this house and the life he had shared with his wife and daughters here. He wants someone who will appreciate it and love it like he did and still does."

I understood his request. The house was important to him as it had become important to me. I would do what I could to make sure his request was realized because it had become my wish as well that someone who loved the house become the new owner. For the first time, I attempted to address Harold directly. I turned my face in the direction I believed him to be based on where Theresa had been talking.

"Harold." I said solemnly. "I assure you that I will pass on your information and your story to whoever the new owner is. I have put a lot of work into this house also and I want the new owners to love it as much as I have. Your work will not go unappreciated and your contributions will not go unknown. You have my word on that."

We stood quietly, waiting for Harold to respond. Of course, I couldn't hear him, but I could tell when Theresa was listening to him. She acted as if she was listening and then she smiled.

"He accepts your word and will now prepare to move on and pass over with Esther."

Again she listened and then she said, "He likes you, Larry. He's sorry he caused you grief. He wants to tell you some more things before he passes on."

"Okay." Was all I could think of to say. What else could there be to tell?

"Apparently," Theresa translated. "Harold likes working with electricity. It's sort of his thing. You had an electrician working in the house during the remodel. Is that correct?"

"Yes, I had two actually. The first one left suddenly so I had to hire another one to finish up."

"Uh huh. I see." She listened some more, beginning to grin as she listened to Harold talk. "I guess the first electrician was doing a terrible job on the electrical work and Harold just couldn't stand it anymore. He just could not allow it to go on. So he scared him away. At the time, he also hoped it would make you leave, but it was more important that the electrician stop hacking up stuff and messing things around."

I chuckled. Harold didn't go into details about what he had done to the poor guy, and I wasn't entirely sure I wanted to know anyway. He must have scared him pretty badly to make him leave all his tools here and never want them back.

"Okay. That explains a lot."

The energy in the room had changed in the last hour. It suddenly felt like we were standing in a room full of our closest friends and family. Like we were gathered for a joyous event or happy get-together of some kind. The air was kind and friendly and some of the chill had left the room. Feeling more comfortable than I had all day with everything that was going on, I asked Harold the burning question.

"Harold, do you know about the money?" I asked in his general direction.

Theresa had no idea what I was talking about, but apparently, Harold did.

"He is not concerned with the money. He does know that you gave it back and he is happy that you found it in your heart to give it to his daughters. But the one thing he is really happy about is the ring."

Theresa looked at me questioningly and I explained the finding of the treasure to her. I told her about all the money and that whole adventure of giving it back to Harold's daughters. Then I told her about the ring, how I had almost thrown it out and had finally found it in my shed and returned it to Rose.

"That meant everything to him." She said. "He had promised that ring to Rose when she was a child and it bothered him immensely that he was not able to tell her where it was before he died. He is very grateful to you for getting that to Rose, where it belonged."

She smiled and laughed as she listened to Harold some more.

"He is mentioning that he reminded you a couple of times about returning the items."

I am guessing that was probably the two times that I found the old money after the original money I found had been removed from the house. I thought about the two times I had found money, in the middle of the floor in the Treasure Room and under the bathtub when demolishing the one upstairs. That must have been Harold's way of reminding me that I still had the money and the ring and that he was getting tired of waiting for me to return it to the daughters.

"He is saying again that he chose you on purpose, that he liked you because he knew that you would be a positive influence, that you would take care of his home and honor his work and his life."

I found that statement very interesting because every time I stepped into that house I felt at home. It was always a comfortable place for me to go even though the remodel was a daunting task, even though there was pressure to get it done and turn it over, even though it reminded me of the stress that was ahead and the fact that the house wasn't selling. I always had peace when I was there. I always felt like I was safe and protected and that everything was going to turn out alright when I was inside the house. Now, I imagine that was Harold's doing. It was his way of making me know that things would be okay, that all would be well.

"Is there anything else you would like to ask Harold?" Theresa questioned when I had been silent for several moments, lost in thought.

I broke from my thoughts and smiled at her.

"No," I said, "I think all my questions have been answered."

She listened again to Harold, or maybe it was Esther, I'm not sure. Then she nodded.

Turning to me, she said, "Are you ready to release them?"

"Yes. What do I have to do?"

"Nothing really. Just take my hand as you did before when we summoned Esther. I'll say the releasing words and then they will be able to pass over gently. That's really all it takes."

"Okay."

Theresa once again took my hand and bowed her head. I closed my eyes and lowered my head as well.

"Ready?" She asked.

"Ready." I said.

"Thank you, Esther, for hearing our call for help. Thank you for coming and meeting with your dear husband, Harold. Thank you for being generous and kind. Harold, thank you for talking with us, for allowing us to speak with you about your options for passing over and thank you for embracing the new life that awaits you on the other side. Your home and your life will continue to be honored here in the physical world as you will continue to honor and love your house and family on the other side."

Taking a deep breath and releasing it slowly, Theresa began the words that would release the spirits back to their afterlives.

"Esther and Harold Bell, we release you. Please return to the other side in peace. We thank you for your assistance and your guidance and we want you to now return to the place and time where you belong. Go in peace and may your spirits be happy ever after."

I felt a breeze, a gentle stirring of air. A cold wind washed over me and opening my eyes, I could see the candles flickered slightly. Although I had not seen them and had not heard them, I had certainly felt them. And now I was certain that Harold and Esther Bell were gone. The room somehow felt empty and drained of its energy. Several of the candles had gone out and Theresa looked exhausted from her efforts.

She squeezed my hand, "They are gone." She said quietly.

I had no words. There was nothing I could say and so I savored the moment, reveling in all that I had gone through that day, all I had experienced, learned and felt. I had never imagined such things could really happen. I never believed in summoning spirits and helping them pass over. I had never experienced anything like it. And now, as I silently helped Theresa put the candles out and gather her things from the basement, I felt like a different man. I felt renewed somehow, like the universe was finally ready to share its truths with me.

We went upstairs. Theresa took her items from the basement into the kitchen to clean them before she put them away in her case. She went through the house, gathering her little plates and the flowers she had used to bless the house. She cleaned those also and I helped her dry them before she put them in her case and zipped it up. I was in awe of what had happened, of all that Theresa was capable of and did every day. What an amazing feeling to help others find closure in such a way.

I locked everything up and walked Theresa out to her car. Helping her put her case away, I shook her hand and thanked her for coming and doing all she had done.

"You did most of it." She said.

"What? You did everything."

"If it hadn't been for your pure heart and your willingness to help Harold, none of it would have happened, Larry. What an amazing journey you have been on these past few months in this house."

She looked back at the house and smiled and then she looked at me.

"I hope you never forget what you have gone through today. I feel that it will have an affect on you for the rest of your life."

"I think you're right." I said. "I definitely feel like a different man than the one that walked through those doors this morning."

We both laughed at that.

I put my hand out to shake hers and she gave me a quick hug instead.

"Call me if you should have the need, Larry. I'm glad to help."

She moved around to the other side of the car and got in. Starting the engine, she waved as she pulled away from the curb.

I walked to my car which was parked in the driveway and opened the door. Standing beside it, I looked at the house and thought about all it represented. A man's life. A connection so strong that he could not pass over without knowing the place would be taken care of by someone who loved it and appreciated his hard work.

His final request prior to him crossing over, was he wanted to make sure that the new buyers would truly appreciate his home and all that he had done in it, that they would share the pride that he had, that they would recognize him and give him the credit he had due for building such a beautiful home and doing everything so perfectly. That house was everything to him.

It was truly amazing to think of the bond between this man and this home. The place where he had loved his wife and raised his children. The building that housed his very soul. I smiled and got in. Even though I knew Harold and Esther were gone, as I backed out of the driveway and pulled away from the house, I waved.

# PART FIVE: THE END

# CHAPTER FOURTEEN

When I got home, I told Sarah everything that had happened. As I relived the day, I was just overwhelmed with the emotion of it all. I cried when I told her how we summoned Esther and the love they had for each other allowed Harold to release his hold on this world and pass on with her into the next. She listened in awe and silence as I told her about Theresa knowing things that she could not have known, about the feeling of someone touching me when no one was there. I told her all of it, everything. When I was finished, she stood in silence. There were just no words to speak. We smiled at each other and hugged.

"Wow," she finally said, "I wish I had been there after all." And we laughed.

The very next weekend we had an open house and we had several people come through the house. I told all of them about the man who had built the house and how he had loved it and raised his family there. I told about the flooding in the basement and other disclosures I had to make. But this time was very different than all the other open houses we had hosted for the house. This time, I felt calm and at ease. I had the overwhelming feeling that it would be okay. That everything would be fine and I didn't need to worry about any of it anymore.

We had a couple of offers come in. They weren't the best of offers. They weren't anything to jump up and down about. It wasn't going to put us in a profit situation but with the market where it was going and as long as we had been on the market without an offer, I decided to negotiate and accept the first offer that came in. By the time it was all said and done, it was still a substantial loss, but not as great a loss as it could have been or would have been if we had continued to hold onto that house for several more months. I just wanted to have that be a closed chapter and move on.

We provided the disclosures to the prospective buyers. We walked the young couple through what had happened and how it was repaired and all the documentation associated with it. They just fell in love with the house, so it worked out rather well and took about four weeks to process and to go into closing. During those four weeks, the couple asked to see the house a few more times. They were making plans for the house. I told them about all the things that Harold had done by hand, the imported Italian marble, the tile and the love and care that had gone into the house. They loved to hear about him and surprisingly, they never did ask me how I knew so much about a man who was passed away. I wouldn't have known what to say anyway.

 #

So my story ends with a loss. It is not the best of situations, but the irony of the whole thing is who would have ever dreamed of investing in a house to flip and going through all we had gone through, all I had gone through. Finding what we found, learning who it belonged to, consulting attorneys, finding the daughters, learning the value of it all and giving it back to them. Who would have thought that a house that contained so much money would cause us to lose money in the end? But we learned a valuable lesson and we had an awesome experience. I truly believe that the blessings far outweigh the negatives and that a pure heart is its own reward.

The positive side is I have this opportunity to share this story with other people so that they can experience what we went through and fantasize and decide for themselves if they would have chosen the same path that we did. I feel good about making the right choice. That is the most important thing for me. I was able to teach my kids a valuable lesson and see their reaction to all of it, their compassion for Harold's daughters and their involvement in returning their inheritance to them. What an amazing experience to be able to do all of that and to share it with those you hold most dear.

The shock and awe that we went through was the experience of a lifetime in and of itself, the excitement and the joy of being able to be a part of that puzzle. What a huge blessing for us to be able to do that, to be able to help those people have closure and for them to get back what belonged to them, what they had been searching for. Was there a lot of fear through out this process? Sure. Is it hard to keep a secret that big? Yeah, it's impossible. If it can be summed up, it is just a matter of adjusting the thoughts and the emotions and channeling those to the right purposes. Once you come to grips with that, then it is semantics. That is all it is from there. It just kicks in.

I will always be proud of the decision that we made. I am not proud of our financial situation, however. I had really made great strides to be in a better financial situation. We were in awesome shape prior to this business venture, but it is not going to wipe us out either. We will recover from the loss we suffered on the house investment. It is going to take some time, but I will get us out of it. I knew how to go about it now, so it wouldn't be hard, just would take some time.

The best part of going through all of that is what an amazing story that I am now able to share with others, to be able to share that experience and show people and reaffirm for people that doing the right thing is not necessarily about you. It is not about your family. It is not about finances, or greed or fear. It's not about panic or stress either. It takes on a whole shape of its own. You don't really understand it until it is over, like most things in life. But we'll be changed and be better for it for the rest of our lives, and I hope everyone that reads this story has a positive experience as well and maybe can take a little bit of that with them through life. We are not special people. We are just regular human beings. We believe in God and we cherish life and we want to help others and be honest and be kind, and that is the bottom line for me, just doing the right thing, living life the way you should live life.

On to the next chapter…

# ABOUT THE AUTHOR

Eileen Maki is a published author in poetry, fiction and non-fiction. Finding a love of reading and writing early on, Eileen has been writing since she was a child and has received several awards for writing both as a child and an adult. With several pieces in publication and always more on the way, Eileen stays busy and loves every minute of it.
She lives in Oregon with her husband, Scott and her boys Jordan and Troy. Eileen loves spending time with her family, writing, reading, crafting and being creative of almost any kind.

Visit Eileen's Website at: www.EileenMaki.com

Or email her at: eileenmaki@gmail.com

Made in the USA
Columbia, SC
21 December 2019